WEAK FOR A COLDHEARTED GOON 2

FATIMA MUNROE

Synopsis

How far will you go when it comes to defending what's yours against those who choose to rip away your happiness for their own selfish gain? Time and time again, Luca has proven to be disloyal to the blood oath he shared with his brothers while expecting their loyalty in return. Sommer has her own set of issues with the Marino brothers, but nonetheless Luca is persistent. What happens when Matteo is finally fed up with his antics?

Everything done in the dark eventually comes to light, and nobody knows this better than Keedra. Toxic relationships are draining enough, but a toxic relationship with a narcissistic parent is enough to send even the sanest person over the edge. During a heated argument, Keedra's mother spews a secret that fractures Keedra's already fragile mental state to pieces. In her emotional turmoil, does she commit the ultimate crime to exact her revenge against Sommer and everyone else who wronged her?

In love, some lines shouldn't be crossed. In the case of true love, all bets are off when the heart wants what it wants. Reno moves in silence while keeping a low profile, but an unexpected relationship with a forbidden love thrusts him in the spotlight. He wanted her first, but in the end, her heart wanted someone else. With time, one love faded while the other grew stronger, thus creating a recipe for destruction in Renato's eyes. Will he risk it all for true love?

When a pretty girl falls in love, she goes through great lengths to protect her heart from the savages. When a savage falls in love with a pretty girl, he falls hard.

Sommer

"What?"

"Shannie is in the hospital, love."

"She—what? Matteo—"

"We at Froedtert. Text me when you downstairs."

I hopped on the Uber app and got a ride to the hospital, my mind running a mile a minute. So many thoughts were going through my brain, but the one that stuck out the most was Shannie in the hospital. Did I want to go up here? Just when I'd come to grips with repairing my relationship with her, this happens. What if I got there and she was already gone? I'd thought about it more than twice over the past few months, but this—this was too much. We never got to…we never…what if my twin was really dead?

The app said the driver was right around the corner, so I rushed downstairs to get up there with Matteo to see what was going on. I didn't know the full details, but I'd find out soon enough. Why was I playing this game of back and forth with Shannie? Why couldn't she understand I only wanted what was best for her, and that wasn't dope? Wait—what was Matteo doing with Shannie? Did she have someone send me that message on—nah. Matteo ain't stupid. He know who he got at home.

That ride to Froedtert was the longest twenty minutes of my life because of traffic; I couldn't get out of that car fast enough. Texting Matteo as I walked, I stepped up to the desk and tried to give the receptionist my name. Just as I opened my mouth to speak, a man near the elevator walked toward me with a hard look in his eye.

"Can I help…Dr. Park? Is everything ok?"

"Uhmm… my husband called—"

"Sommer?" the man interrupted while I fumbled over my words. For some reason what I wanted to say wasn't reaching my lips.

"Yes."

"Matteo told me to bring you upstairs when you got here. Follow me." He turned and began walking toward the elevator as I nodded at the receptionist. She nodded and went back to answering phones. The elevator dinged, and we both got on. Words formed in my mind, but nothing came out while I absently watched the man push the button for the fifth floor. Staring silently at the numbers as they lit up from left to right, something deep in the pit of my stomach told me it was only a matter of time before—I brushed off the thought before it fully materialized, praying the heaviness in my heart was from what I read prior to Matteo's phone call or even my father's vague text and not from my sister's impending death.

Scurrying off the elevator when it stopped and the doors slowly slid open, I looked around urgently for him. I needed to hear his words, I needed to hear Matteo tell me everything was ok and the phone call was just a precaution. Doctors did that all the time, right? I know I did. Maybe she'd stabilized on my way here. Maybe she woke up, and—"Baby, what are the doctors saying?" I questioned when I bumped into him on my way to the waiting room. "Is there an update?"

"Sommer…" His arms wrapped around me slowly, palming the back of my head to rest against his neck.

"No... Matteo don't say that! Don't say—" Tears welled up in my orbs, even though I wasn't a mind reader.

"They say it's only a matter of time, love. Follow me, she's in the ICU." He took my hand and led me to the window, where I was regulated to watching my sister slip away from behind the thick double-paned glass.

"We can't go in? I gotta—" I wanted to see her chart...there had to be something else I could do instead of helplessly palm the glass as my living reflection laid on the plastic and foam mattress looking devoid of life. "Shannie," I whispered, my breath created a light fog on the window.

"Come on, love. We gotta put on these masks and gowns after we wash up first. The area is sterile." Matteo had to direct my actions because I was a mess. We got cleaned up, and covered from head to toe in masks, gowns, and gloves, went inside to see my sister.

"Shannie? I know you can't speak, but I need you to listen to me. I love you." I spoke from my heart with a trembling bottom lip. "I love you. Don't leave me, Shannie. I promise I'll be a better sister to you. We gonna get you some help. Just please… don't leave me. Shannie, please don't… I'll be alone." I dropped to one knee and whispered in her ear, "I'll be alone, Shannie. Please don't leave me with memories… I need you. I'm pregnant. Your niece or nephew needs you. Please, sis." I kissed the side of her head, my tears ran in dirty rivers down the side of her face.

"Sommer. Love of my life." Matteo gently touched my elbow. "The doctors are doing everything they can—"

When the machines began to beep loudly, I lost it. I looked over and focused on the one regulating her breathing, watching the digitized lines drag across the small screen in high peaks with long valleys. Her heart rate was dropping before her body began going into convulsions; Shannie was so small I was so scared she would break in two each time she slammed against the mattress. "NOOOO! SHANNIE! HELP ME, SOMEBODY PLEASE HELP ME!" I screamed before starting chest compressions and CPR.

Matteo pulled me out of the room once the hospital staff ran down the hallway and flooded her space, working frantically to stop her from leaving me, but seeing the look on the doctor's face as the nurse pulled the shade down, I knew it was too late. I could never go back and say the things I left unsaid. We could never sit around the table and reminisce on the old days. Never would my baby meet his or her only aunt. Once again, our timing was off. "It's too late," I wept on Matteo's shoulder while he consoled my pain.

Matteo

Even though they were twins, even though they didn't really fuck with each other like that, Sommer was still an emotional wreck seeing her sister leave this earth in front of her. Even as a doctor, it wasn't nothing she could've done to stop it, unless she intervened when Shannie took that first inhale of powder. With her twin's death, I knew she felt like she was left in the world by herself, and that fucked with me probably as much as it did her. I needed her to understand I was her family. She still had me. Maybe not Luca and probably half of Renato, but Sommer had me for the long haul.

The last person I cared about who died was my mother, so naturally I went into protective mode when it came to mine. After I took her home, I gave her a bath and made

sure she was good before I went back to the
hospital to make arrangements for Shannie's
funeral. Regardless of the life she lived, I
had to make sure she went out in style. My
sister-in-law was going to have the biggest
going-home party the city ever saw.
Considering what she'd gone through in life,
she deserved that.

"Matteo, is that you?" Sommer called out
after I got home for the second time. I gotta
admit, it felt good coming home to someone
who loved you unconditionally with no
strings attached. She made me want to do
right by her and come home before twelve.

"Yeah, it's me."

I heard her footfalls on the floor above
my head and hung my coat up in the foyer
before meeting her halfway on the steps.
"Matteo?"

"Yes love?"

"Who you got pregnant?"

"Who I—what?"

"You heard me!" Her screams were so loud she shook the picture frames on the walls. "Who you got pregnant, Matteo!"

"I ain't—"

"You lying." She turned and stomped back up the steps. "YOU LYING MATTEO! It's good though. You and your baby mama can live here in this fucking house—"

"Sommer, wait!" I jogged up two steps before tripping on the third. She was moving so fast I could barely catch up with her. "STOP, DAMMIT!"

"OH, now we CUSSING at each other, huh! My name ain't dammit!"

"Sommer—"

"Why, God? Why did I have to lose my only family and the one man You sent to me all in the same day!" she wailed, and all I could to was try to calm her down. "Don't worry, I'll be ok though." She disappeared for a few seconds into our dark bedroom, reappearing with a suitcase. "I left everything you bought me! You can have it! Give it to whoever out here sending me sonograms, talking 'bout 'congrats step mama'! Fuck you, fuck her, and fuck that damn baby!"

"Sommer, stop!" I grabbed her by the arm as she tried to push past me. "I swear to God I have no idea what you talking about!"

"Hmph, you don't know what I'm talking about, Matteo? You got somebody pregnant and don't know who she is? That tells me you and ya little head just do whatever y'all want with no consequences, huh!" she stared up at me with tears in her eyes. I raised a hand to wipe them away, but she smacked my arm in mid-air. "Don't touch me! Get out of my way!"

I didn't have a leg to stand on, she'd already made up her mind, and there was nothing I could do to change it. I let her think for too long. She said something when she called, and I told her Shannie was in the hospital. We hadn't talked about it since, and coupled with her sister's death, mentally, she was on a thousand. "Who told you I got them pregnant, Sommer? Just tell me that!"

"Oh, go check your bedroom, love," she spat with honey-coated sarcasm. "Everything you need to know is right there, sweetie. Now please move outta my way!"

"Sommer, let's talk—"

"MOVE, MATTEO!"

I threw my hands up in the air so she could get past, checking my phone in the process. If she thought she was just gonna walk out of my life without allowing me to explain myself, she had me fucked up.

"Who coming to pick you up, Sommer? Ain't no driver on his way out here according to the app!"

"Hmph. You think I need your little Uber app to get around?" she smiled cunningly. "I got somebody else coming to get me."

"Who picking you up, Sommer? You betta not have a nigga coming out here to get you from my fucking house!" I yelled as she answered her phone.

"Yeah, I'm ready. You outside? Ok, I'm coming now," she smirked before hitting end on her phone. "No, Matteo, I don't have 'some nigga' coming to pick me up."

I saw the headlights pull into my circular driveway and grabbed the .9 millimeter Glock from my waistband, sliding the safety off. "You gave a muthafucka my gate code, and now he sitting in front of my house waiting on you? After I kill this nigga, yo' ass is next!"

The door swung open, and the last man I expected to see stood in my doorway with the biggest smile on his face, reaching for her suitcase. "Sommer, you ready?"

"Yeah. Can you put my bag in the trunk please?" she spoke sweetly as he moved out the way for her to walk out of my life.

"I gotchu."

"Reno? Fuck is you doing at my house picking up my wife?"

"First and foremost, Matteo, don't flex on me like I won't shoot yo' old ass first," he pointed when he saw my piece in hand. "Second, this ain't what it looks like. I'm taking Sommer somewhere so she can cool down, considering her physical and mental state. Third, call Luca. He gotta talk to you about something." Nodding in my direction, he grabbed Sommer's suitcase and left me standing on my own steps confused.

I didn't know Sommer knew Reno, much less trusted him enough to call him when she was pissed off at me. Not gonna lie, I thought it was Luca coming through that door, because I was about to shoot him in the ankle. But Reno? "The hell going on around here?" I mumbled aloud, watching his taillights disappear behind the bushes in front of my circular driveway.

I jogged up the steps to see what was in my bedroom and was met with hundreds of pictures of a sonogram taped to the bed. The walls were completely covered as high up as she could reach. The dressers were replaced with paper, as well as the mirrors and the doors. She even had this pic taped all over my bathroom, lined up in perfect squares. Oh, my baby had time today; she had my bathtub covered and replaced my shower curtains with this kid. Opening my closet, I saw she had the pics taped on the other side of the door and pinned on the hangers with my clothes. She taped at least five pic to my shoeboxes. Snatching one of the photos down, I stared at the screenshot:

Facebook User: *Congrats, step mama. Look like we gonna be one big, happy family after all. LOLOLOLOLOLOL!*

Step mama? One big, happy family after… these people 'bout to make me kill some fucking body. Grabbing my phone from my pocket, I hit talk on Luca's number. "Matteo."

"Where Keedra at?"

"In a basement on 104th. Why?"

"Text me the address," I growled before hanging up. This whole day had her name written all over it. I knew it was a calm before the storm, but I wasn't ready for Hurricane Keedra. *That's aight. She seemed to have forgotten who the fuck I am,* I mumbled, changing into some black skinny jogging pants with matching tee shirt and Nikes before I headed back out in the streets. This bitch was begging for my attention, so I was about to give it to her.

Keedra

My mama cooked a big dinner of meatloaf, fried chicken, spinach and cheese stuffed shells, mashed potatoes, green beans, candied yams, Hawaiian rolls, and a peach cobbler with homemade lemonade. I got two plates of everything before I went in my room to lie down for a while. Since I didn't catch Matteo earlier, I was trying to hopefully run into him tonight while he was on the block.

I'd just tucked my head into my pillow and dozed off when my mama knocked on my door. "Keedra. Somebody at the front door for you."

"Who is it, Mama?" I tried to squint the sleep out of my eyes, blinking a few times so I could see.

"Keedra, I done told you before, I ain't yo' damn butler. Come find out!"

Blinking my surroundings clear, I rolled my eyes to the ceiling before focusing back on the door. Taking a deep breath in, I threw the covers off me and stood up to stretch while exhaling. I couldn't wait until Matteo—until I got out of this house. I had to get out of this house first.

With sleep still in my eyes, I rubbed my lids while padding through the dark front room, almost tripping over the table in the middle of the floor. Mama called herself changing the living room around for the fifth time this month, and that shit was still ugly. Feng Shui my ass; what she really needed was a better set of eyes to see how trifling her house really was. *Whew, chile...* I mused to myself.

Shuffling from my bedroom to the front door, I pulled it open and saw nothing but a dark shadow on the porch. Of course my first instinct was to run my hand along the wall next to the door to turn on the porch light, but gave up on once I realized the bulb was blown. "Who is that?"

"Keedra."

"Yea."

The figure reached out and pulled me out the house by my neck, covering my nose and mouth with a cloth as I opened my mouth… to… screeeeeeeeeammmmm…

§

"Luca? Is that—"

Smack!

My head snapped hard to the right, hair slapping my face. Pins and needles stung my skin while I sat in the dimly lit room confused. Sweat seeped out of my pores as I tried to wiggle my hands free from the cords wrapped around my wrists.

"Aye, go tell the boss this bitch woke," a dark shadow spoke sardonically as his body lumbered through the door. "She smell good too. If he letting us fuck, I'm first."

I heard a group of men laughing just outside the door, but none of them sounded even remotely familiar. *Who is their boss?* I wondered. *And why did he need to kidnap me?*

"My first mind said for me to kill yo' spiteful ass." Matteo's voice came through the door. His heavy footfalls moved adroitly to where I sat in shock. "Giving a crackhead battery acid because you thought that was my wife was a bitch move. That's how I knew it was you. Sending the wife that message though?" I saw his head nod up and down against the dull light streaming in from outside of the room as he began clapping slowly. "Bet you didn't bank on that jealous shit getting your throat slit, did you?"

"Matteo, I-I swear I don't know what you're talking about!" I lied. Now that battery acid... that was all me. I didn't send any messages. At least not me personally.

"I see your selective memory has kicked in, so allow me the opportunity to refresh you on a few things." Pulling up a chair on my right side, he sat so close I could smell the Versace soap coming from his neck. "Last time we talked, you called yourself taking me down memory lane. Let's go back, shall we?"

"Matteo—"

"Remember your little friend, Maritza? The one you grew up with that you told you lived with me? Remember she called herself breaking in my trap house, and you covered for her?" his lips rubbed against my earlobe as tears rolled down my face.

"Maritza was my best friend, Matteo. My best friend in the whole world, she genuinely loved me for—"

"She genuinely loved you for fucking with me so she could smoke for free," he interrupted. "Remember? I still got her on camera with one hand on Vito's dick and the other hand grabbing an ounce of coke off the table. Remember? The bitch had been stealing from me for two months before your stupid ass even mentioned she was fucking with one of my people. You remember her, right? Your best friend. Maritza."

"Matteo, you didn't have to—"

"What have I always told you, Keedra? What was my number one rule when people started fucking with my livelihood? Surely you remember that." He grabbed a handful of my hair and snapped my head back, still growling in my ear.

"Bitches bleed just like us," I mumbled low enough for us to hear.

"Come on now baby, I know you louder than that," he chuckled darkly, tightening his grip before pulling a knife out his pocket. Dragging the serrated edges across my throat, he tugged harder on my tresses; I really thought my neck snapped.

"Bitches bleed just like us, Matteo!"

"Bitches bleed just like us," he whispered sinisterly. "In Maritza's case, she just— hmm… exploded. All over the place," he taunted, triggering memories of me finding her dead body rotting in the living room of her apartment. "That battery acid is a muthafucka, ain't it?"

"Matteo, I swear, I didn't—"

"See if you knew what you was doing, you'd know a crackhead samples the dope first. They not just gonna jump out the gate with new product from somebody they don't know. Even fiends like that top quality shit, wanna make sure that high gonna take them where they need to go," Matteo put me up on game while scraping the blade back and forth across my neck. "Had you mixed it with a little something, it might've done exactly what you wanted it to do just like that," the snapping of his fingers so close to my ear made me jump. "Oh yeah, I dropped that little baggie I found on the floor off at the lab so they could run fingerprint testing to see exactly who all touched it. Now I'm sure I'll find a couple of sets of fingerprints, but what if—" he rested the point of the knife against the base of my neck and began applying pressure. "—what if one of those fingerprints belongs to my little Keedra?"

"Matteo, it-it was an accident! I-I thought—"

"Wife is an identical twin," he revealed. "You thought I was fucking a crackhead, didn't you?"

"Matteo—"

"You always was a dumb lil' bitch," he spat through gritted teeth. "Always trying to be a dope girl, always trying to keep up with the Marino boys. Always thinking you could do shit behind my back that I wouldn't find out about. Bitch, you hustling backward; if I wanted a hood bitch, I'd have one. I already knocked down half ya friends, what make you think I wanted you, Keedra?"

My blood was boiling; I hadn't heard one word he said because the more I thought about it, the more I realized the only reason I was in this basement was because his precious Sommer was upset. "Matteo, you married her? You married her, Matteo!" I yelled, unable to control my emotions. He kept referring to this woman as his 'wife'.

We'd been in the same house for almost five years and half the time I was sleeping in the guest bedroom, but she comes along and now he ready to settle down? I got the D a few months ago in his front room. He couldn't have been *that* much in love.

"To be somebody with a whole knife to their throat, you asking the wrong questions," he spoke quietly, twisting the knife harder into my skin. I felt a warm trickle of blood winding down my chest. "But because I'm feeling generous, I'll answer your question. Not yet, but it's coming. Speaking of which, bitch, you pregnant?"

"Pregnant? Why would you ask me that?"

"So you still pretending like you ain't send that Facebook message, huh?"

"Matteo, I swear—"

"You just swore you didn't give Shannie that baggie of battery acid either. Your word ain't worth shit no more."

"Matteo, please! Yes, I was mad at Shannie, Sommer, whatever her name is—"

Smack!

"You know her name! Don't start that shit!"

"Sommer! I was mad at Sommer! But I promise you, Matteo, I didn't send her a message on nothing!"

Matteo wiped his finger across the blood seeping from the puncture wound in my neck, pressing the digit forcefully to my lips. "Bitches bleed just like us, Keedra."

I parted my lips slightly, the metallic taste of blood filled my mouth as he looked on. "Next time you gotta piss, call X. We'll see if yo' lil' stupid ass pregnant or not. I'll tell you this though; if you are, I hope you made peace with whoever your god is. You'll be meeting him soon enough."

"You'll kill your own baby, Matteo?"

"My baby?" he fumed, mushing my head. "Bitch, that could be my baby, my nephew, Jerry's kid—"

Jerry? How did he know about Jerry?
"Jerry? I don't know anybody named Jerry."

"Oh, now you don't know the person who got your debut video took down off of Pornhub?"

"Wait—that wasn't you who got the video removed?"

Matteo's intense stare cut right through me; even if the light prevented me from seeing his piercing brown eyes, I felt it. "We done, Keedra. You hear me? We done. I catch you contacting my wife again, this conversation won't be as friendly."

I took a deep breath in and released it slowly, relieved. Knowing Matteo's temper,

I was surprised I was still alive. After all, he did murder my best friend with a baggie of battery acid he told her was heroin. "Thank you, Matteo. Thank you so—AAAHHH!" The knife point slammed through my hand, piercing my skin with the rage he made a point to convey. The palm of my hand ripped open, pinning me to the arm of the chair in the process. My hand swelled up quickly once the steel smashed through my bones, rearranging my veins as blood poured from the open wound.

"Bitches bleed just like us, Keedra. Don't forget that," he remarked darkly before he stood up, dusting off his pants. "X! Catch this bitch's piss next time she go, if she piss in this chair, slit her fucking throat!"

"I got'chu chief!" I heard X's response, hoping to wiggle the knife from my bound wrist trying to remove it from my palm.

"I love an efficient nigga," Matteo mumbled, more to himself than me while I watched him walk calmly out the room. Dizzy from the intense pain shooting through my hand, my head began to pound slowly. Dark and fuzzy figures swam back and forth in front of my peripheral vision until I eventually passed out.

Luca

Me and my brother still had to have that conversation about what I did, but I gave him his space. He needed to be there to console ol' girl through the loss of her sister. In the meantime, I sent X and a couple other goons from the block to Keedra's house so she could have a 'chat' with the love of her life. Matteo was gonna either kill that girl or make her wish she was dead.

I stepped into Matteo's side of the business since he was otherwise occupied. Reno texted me a while ago, telling me to call first before I came over because he had company. Now that was more intriguing than anything; Reno didn't have company. We knew he did his thing out here, but he didn't have women running in and out of his house like we did. I take that back, like I did. Matteo been wifed up for a minute;

even if he wasn't claiming Keedra he still didn't bring people to his crib like that. Everybody knew where the trap house was though.

"Aye," I answered my phone from the Bluetooth button on my steering wheel. "What's up with ya people?"

"Luca Marino." Jerry greeted me cheerily through the car's speakers. "I was just about to ask you the same thing."

"What he say?"

"Luca, you know Matteo already knows about our little partnership, right? Just introduce him to David so we can go back to making this money."

Jerry was always fucking some shit up. If Matteo knew about what I had going on… "Which one?"

"The one between you and our little friend with the diamonds."

"Matteo don't know about David."

"We've had a conversation recently about you and David. Matteo knows."

"You talked to my brother about—"

"Listen, Luca. This isn't about you, your brother, or none of that other shit. This is about making a shitload of money for the rest of our lives. Regardless of where it comes from, all money spends whether you selling dope, diamonds, pussy, or letting somebody tap that booty hole. Now I don't know about you, but I'll sell my wife's pussy to the highest bidder and ask how big the dick was as long as I got paid. I've made nice with David, all you have to do is show up to Potawatomie with Matteo and we can go back to making this money. Are you in or out?"

I hadn't put any money in the family account since David walked away from me that afternoon at the same hotel this meeting was supposed to be happening at. Matteo hadn't said anything, but I knew it was only a matter of time before he started asking questions, especially since Xander was one of his go to men in the streets. He had to know Tamra wasn't doing the IG thing anymore with her doctor putting her on bed rest until she had the baby. I could do it myself, I just didn't have the patience to be in the house all day on the internet like that.

"I'm in." I replied, slightly apprehensive seeing Matteo's number come through on the other line. "Text me the addy, we'll be there." I clicked over and braced myself for whatever he had to say. Not only did Matteo know about the partnership, I didn't know how long he knew. With Shannie dead and Keedra tied up in a basement, ain't no telling what kind of mood he was in. "Matteo."

"What we gotta talk about, Luca Marino?"

"Who said—"

"Reno told me to call you." My brother was already interrupting mid-sentence, which meant he wasn't with the shits. "Meet me."

"Where?"

"How about… let's see… Potawatomie in about an hour. You free?"

"Yeah, I'm free," I responded, confused. Matteo didn't gamble. "We hitting the tables?"

"Meet me at the bar."

"I'll be there—Matteo?" I looked over at the console and saw he'd hung up. Shaking my head, I knew I had to get my mind in the game when Jerry's text flashed on the screen. We were supposed to be meeting up with David at Potawatomie in an hour. "This nigga…" I mumbled , starting up the Jag before peeling off down the street.

§

Jerry and David were sitting at the table laughing when I walked in, the smoke from their expensive cigars curling diaphanously around their empty shot glasses. Matteo sat at the bar with a brooding look, his eyes darting back and forth from the men to the door and back again. Adjusting the lapel on my suit, I headed in my brother's direction as Jerry showed David something on his phone. "Matteo."

"I'ma ask you one more time before I go over here to this table and fuck with these two sheisty muthafuckas. What you got to tell me, Luca Marino?"

"So much shit been going on I just haven't had the chance—"

"Yo' ass always got something to say when it come to Sommer, but when I ask you a simple question, you always beating around the bush," he threw back his shot of brown liquor, wiping his mouth with the back of his hand. "If you kept yo' head in the game instead of tryna play that jealous shit, you'd know yo' dumb ass made a deal with the fucking devil that I gotta get us the fuck out of!"

"Matteo, who the fuck you talkin' to?"

"You don't want me to answer that right now, so I suggest you bring yo' ass over here to this table," he stood nose to nose with me, eyes black as night.

Watching him take long strides to where my business partners sat, Matteo headed over to the table. Both men stood up and showed respect as my brother sat down. Taking the seat near him, I made myself comfortable in my seat as Matteo sat back, showing off the handle to his .9 millimeter pistol against his black tee and jeans while staring both men in the eye. "Why am I here?" he began, sucking his teeth.

"Matteo Marino. I've heard many good things about you." David reached across the small table, extending his hand to shake. Matteo stared at his hand for a second before resuming his stance.

"Yet I've heard nothing about you. If you and my brother already concocted this scheme behind my back, why do we need to meet again?"

"You don't know who I am, do you?"

"We ain't bout to go back and forth." Matteo stood up and reached for his pistol. "I don't give a fuck who you are. Luca ain't doing no fucking business with you, him, or no damn body else unless I say so!" He pointed the gun back and forth between both men, settling on aiming the barrel at David's head as a woman sitting near us looked over and let out a blood curdling scream. Security started heading our way, tasers drawn, as if that was supposed to scare us.

"You really gonna shoot your own father?" David scoffed vehemently, lighting his cigar for a second time and taking a long pull. I saw movement from my peripheral vision, chairs scraped across the tiled floors trying to get away from where we sat calmly.

"Nigga, you ain't shit to me. My pops been in the ground for a long time now." Matteo cocked his pistol before resting the tip directly between David's eyes.

"Tamiko never told you about me, I see. Ask her how she knows Jerry," he slid his eyes back and forth between my brother and the man sitting next to him looking slightly uncomfortable.

"You know what they say about speaking ill of the dead." Matteo warned, his finger curled around the pistol's trigger. Before I could react, a security guard tackled him to the ground from behind, trying to be a hero.

My brother stumbled slightly, falling to one knee when I caught the man around his neck and choked him out. "GET THE FUCK OFF ME, BITCH!"

"John, what are you doing? Do you know who his wife is!" the front desk clerk screamed, running over to where we were with a cordless phone in hand. "Mr. Marino, I'm so sorry, but for the safety of our other guests, we cannot allow you back at the hotel. We'll comp your stay—"

"My wife ain't staying in this shithole!" Matteo roared, jumping to his feet once he saw me let the man go. "And you buried yourself when you put yo' muthafuckin' hands on me, rent-a-cop muthafucka!" The security guard stood gasping for air when Matteo swung and punched him in the face. His body swiftly hit the ground; my brother knocked him out cold. "Luca, end this shit now! And David, you can eat a dick! Fuck away from me!" Matteo thundered, his voice echoing from the walls as he took long strides toward the sliding glass doors.

"Luca, I hate that—"

"Stay the fuck away from us, bitch!" I spat, tossing a few bills on the table for the drinks before following my brother's lead. Matteo was right; I made a deal with the devil over money and pussy, and now that deal was coming back to fuck with me with a vengeance. The only other person still living who knew our mother's name was Renato. "This can't be fucking life, man. It can't."

Reno

"Matteo, you do realize you asking me to remember some shit that happened back when I was a kid, right? How the fuck am I supposed to know who was in that room and what they talked about?" I yelled at my brother while the makings of a headache began throbbing at the base of my skull.

"Reno, I know you blocked that day out in your head. I know. I need you to think though. It's important. Who all was in the room the day Pops died?"

I sat back in my recliner, sighing hard as I tried to remember who was there. Sommer brought me two pain pills and a cup of water before disappearing again out of the office where I sat pondering Matteo's question. "Shit's blurry, bro."

"Was Jerry there?"

"Jerry… Jerry… you talking 'bout Sleazo?"

"That's exactly who I'm talking 'bout."

"Why would he have been at our house?"

"Reno, was he there or not?"

"Uhmm… maybe? Matteo, I dead ass don't remember. Been blocking that day out for years now."

"Aight, lil' bro. Do me a favor though, think on it and let me know. How's the wife doing?"

"She good. I might keep her around for a little while." I cackled, knowing he was pissed she left in the first place.

"You might keep her around, huh. Reno how you know Sommer, man? I'm really talking myself out of killing yo' ass."

"I came over to the house one day looking for something, and she was there with the designer. Funny, because the designer thought I was you until she started screaming. I almost had to break her fingers to stop her from calling the police!"

"You do know Sommer Park is the best doctor in southeast Wisconsin, right?"

"I know now." Renato pulled up an article where USA Today featured her little clinic in the hood on the front page. "Why you ain't say nothing?"

"She asked me not to. Baby be tryna act like me, like she a hood nigga. I had to tell her that's not who I fell in love with. She getting back to the shy little brown skin from the 'burbs. That's my baby."

"I figured. Aye, you look good with a real one on ya' arm."

"Get you one too, we can look like twins," he chuckled. "Did you find what you were looking for?"

"Keedra said something about a bag she left at your house a few months ago?"

Matteo huffed, grabbing himself a cigar from the humidor. "Y'all stop letting Keedra talk that shit," he spoke gruffly before striking the match against the table to light his cigar. "She ain't got nothing at my house."

I stared at him sideways for a second before turning my lips up at his in love ass. "Woman stay with you for five years, you put her out in thirty minutes, and she ain't got NOTHING at ya' house, bro? I find that hard to believe."

"Speaking of Keedra, she said anything to you about being pregnant?"

"No, Matteo, NO!" My skull started pounding when he said 'Keedra' and 'pregnant' in the same sentence. "That's NOT who you—"

"Reno, I was just about to say if she did, it ain't mine, bro," we dapped up as the headache subsided. "With everything else going on, I ain't got time to be dealing with no baby mama unless the one in the house with me pregnant. And when she is, I'm wifing her right up. Y'all ain't gotta worry about me and Keedra."

"That's why you don't bring everybody to ya' house, Matteo. Ain't no telling—"

"Look, Pop." Matteo chided, he always referred to me as his father when I started speaking facts. "Only woman ever been to my house other than thot box is Sommer." He sat back for a few minutes, puffing on his cigar thoughtfully. "Aye, you think Keedra pregnant?"

"We all know why Keedra ain't pregnant," I chuckled.

"Why not?"

"Keedra bisexual. A baby would interfere with her current lifestyle."

"She what?"

"After you put her out, I saw her going into this one club downtown that's known for—"

"Keedra ain't bisexual. If she was, she should've been said something. Probably would still be at the house," he laughed quietly to himself. "My girl got a girlfriend," he sang lowly.

"Aye, back to Sleazo. What's going on with him and Pop?"

"I don't know. Shit ain't making sense right now. Aye, I'm 'bout to go upstairs and lay down for a minute before I go home."

I don't know who he thought he was talking to, but I knew my brother. His woman was here, it was late, and he was still full of adrenaline from what he'd just found out at the hotel. "Sommer sleep, Matteo."

"How you know?"

"She said she was 'bout to go to bed."

"Oh, well in that case, I'll sleep on the couch then."

"Couch, huh."

"Yeah."

I laughed watching him stand up and fake stretch, like he could barely walk. "Let that woman get some rest, Matteo."

"Fuck that. I got a house she can sleep at just fine."

By the time I realized what he was doing, he was already halfway up the steps.

"Matteo!"

"What, Reno!"

"Second room on the left."

"Aight."

Sommer

After ten days overseas, putting my name on his house, redecorating everything, giving this man my heart... I check my inbox and see an anonymous message about me being somebody's step mama? Nah, Matteo had to tell me something. I just found out about my own pregnancy. What I look like; a doctor taking care of two babies, and one of 'em ain't mine?

All these women who say the baby's innocent and it ain't their fault the man cheated... yes it is. Because if it wasn't for that baby, it wouldn't be tension in the house where his woman was trying to make a home for her and her man. From what I could see, side chicks seemed to think that baby gave her a say in that man's life. I ain't the one who gonna have nobody's kid running my household, talking 'bout I can't discipline him because 'his mama said so'. We ain't even gonna talk about the games women play when they knew the man had a woman and pursued him anyway. Nah. Like I told Matteo, fuck a baby. He better be a father to mine and mine ONLY.

A distraction was what I needed, so I reached out to my dad for guidance. We still needed to talk about the text he sent anyway, so I hit talk on his number and waited for him to answer. "Hi Daddy."

"Hey pumpkin. Did you get my message?"

"Yes. Who is Tamiko?"

Dad sighed deeply, pausing for a few seconds before he spoke. "Your mom decided to talk, but she still didn't give me too much information on your real parents. She said Tamiko was her best friend, and if anybody would know anything about what was going on in the city back then, she'd know."

"Do you know her?"

"Unfortunately baby girl, I wasn't privy to what your mother had going on in Milwaukee. She had a separate persona whom I've never met. I'm sorry, baby."

"No worries, Daddy. I'll ask around the clinic and see if I can find anyone who knows her. Hopefully she can give me some answers about why Shannie and I didn't grow up together."

"Who is Shannie?"

"My twin." I forgot in my haste, I hadn't given my parents any details about the woman I shared a face with, only screaming her existence when I found out on that cold winter day. "Her name is Shannie Tyler."

"Was she—" Daddy stopped to clear his throat. "—'adopted' too?"

"From what I can tell, no. She had a hard life, Daddy. I don't know what she's gone through in her life, but my colleagues at the hospital say she's been on hard drugs for at least seventeen years."

"Baby girl, if she's your twin, that means—"

"She's been using drugs since middle school. I know Daddy."

"I don't know if you'll ever forgive your mother," Daddy sighed. "But if you can find it in your heart, please do so. For me."

"I've already forgiven her, Daddy."

"Thank you, pumpkin."

We talked for a few more minutes before he hung up. Holding the phone to my chest, I took a few minutes to think about what my life could've been had me and my sister grew up together. Would I be strung out on drugs, not caring whether I lived or died, as long as I could chase my next high? Would

Matteo have killed me right along with my sister? Who were our parents? Did anyone know anything?

Everything was hitting me all at once, and I was tired. Shannie flat lining in the O.R. would be burned in my memory for the rest of my life, whether I wanted it to be or not. My mother's unwillingness to tell me who my biological parents were would haunt me until I knew the truth. That sonogram in my DM gave me chills; I couldn't be in that house with Matteo again. Overall, I was generally calm, nothing fazed me. That sonogram fazed the hell out of me though.

I'd just dozed off from crying myself to sleep when I thought I heard a noise outside my bedroom door. Waiting to see if Reno was on the other side, I tucked my head in and was somewhere between fully woke and half asleep when the door opened quietly and shut. He must've been looking for something—

"Say what you want... but don't say it's overrrr. Call me out my name... but don't say you over meeee..." Usher's 'Say What You Want' was being serenaded softly in my ear by the man who could easily be the love of my life. "You leaving me, Sommer?"

"Yup. Go home, Matteo."

"I am home. You my home. Scoot over." Nudging me to the other side of the bed, Matteo slid under the covers and wrapped his arms around my waist. "You smell good."

"You don't."

"What I smell like?"

"Pussy," I lied. My man smelled good. He still had his signature Versace scent, but there was something else... he smelled like alcohol... some of 'that good kush' he

usually smoked before we met up... anger...
rage...adrenaline. Whatever it was had me
wanting him in the worst way. Yeah, I was
hurt, but he needed to take that hurt away
the way that only he knew how.

"You a lie. Your man don't smell like no
damn pussy. Liquor, maybe. Lil' bit of that
premium blueberry kush...yea, probably. I
know for a fact I don't smell like no fuckin'
pussy though."

"Lemme see." I rolled over and was face
to face with his hard chest.

"Gimme your hand." Skin to skin along
his naked thigh, he wrapped my fingers
around his dick. "That's all you, Sommer.
He don't even get hard for none of these
bitches out here."

"But you pregnant though." I snatched
away from his grip to prove a point. If we
kept touching we was gonna end up in a
sticky situation both of us would love.

"Don't be pulling away from me. You know I'ma touchy boyfriend; I like grabbing your ass…" he squeezed my booty cheek. "…rubbing yo' thighs…" he slowly ran his hand from the top to the bottom of my thigh. "…grabbing yo' titties…" he grazed my nipples with his fingertips before gripping a handful of my mounds, "…and feeling that pussy," he mumbled with his hand traveling to my inner thigh, resting his hand between my legs with the thin material stopping him from sliding his fingers inside my gushy box. "You so fucking wet. She miss me. Mmhmm… she miss Matteo, don't she," he mumbled, diving underneath the covers.

"I got people in my inbox telling me we sharing some D, yet you think you can just touch my coochie and make everything better?" I scooted away from his touchy feely self. The moonlight hit his face through the curtains once he reappeared from underneath the covers looking all fake hurt.

"Sommer, on my life, I don't know who sent you that message. Soon as I find out who did though—"

"No, Matteo. You don't understand. You're pregnant, but not by the sonogram stalker." It was my turn to grab his hand and placed it on my belly. "I gotta go to the—"

"What? When?" he questioned, touching his forehead to mine.

"I don't know, but if I had to guess it was probably that first time we…"

Matteo gripped my face with both hands and pulled me to him, softly slipping his tongue between my lips. The anger from earlier melted away when I wrapped my hand around his neck and legs around his naked body. "I love you Sommer Marino," he mumbled, edging my panties to the side before he slid inside my pregnant pocket.

"Mmm… how you mad at me with yo' pussy this wet?"

"You make me sick, Matteo," I moaned, already on top of him. Gripping my hips, he was heaven snaking in and out of my wetness, gently stroking my nub while my hips gyrated left to right.

"You love me, Sommer," he grunted, sweat slick and tempting…I begged myself not to run my tongue along his massive pectorals. "Stop acting like you don't."

"Oouu, I hate you, Matteo Marino," I whimpered. Matteo put one hand behind him for balance and bounced my little self up and down, my skin smacking rhythmically against his. "I hate you so fucking—"

"Cum on him," he ordered. "If this yo' muthafuckin' dick, you betta cum on him right fuckin'—"

Just like every other time he had me speaking in tongues, my orgasm happily sprung forth when he called.

"MATTEOOOOO!"

"Mmhmm… she love me. Say you love me, dammit!"

"I-I love—"

"Say it like I taught you that first night, or I'll take him back!"

"I LOVE YOU MATTEO MARINO!"

"You betta fuckin' love me," he buried his face n the crook of my neck, continuing his relentless tapping the bottom of my pussy with the tip of his dick. "I love yo' ass, you betta not ever say you hate me, you hear me Sommer?"

"Mmhmm—"

"Daddy gonna have to punish you again, you don't want that, do you?" Matteo gently rested my head on the pillow before he grabbed my ankles and pushed them to the side of my head, pinning me to the mattress.

"MATTEOOO—AAAHHH!"

"Stop crying and take this dick, you hurt my feelings," he moaned in my ear. "Telling me you hate me, knowing how much I love you," he slowed his stroke and made love to my pussy. "I gave you my baby, gotcho ass didn't I? Hold yo' muthafucking ankles!"

"That's why you make me sick— MATTEO!" I did as I was told, watching him balance himself before angling his dick downward and quickly slipped inside my gushy. My man gripped my waist and started banging my guts with precision like he hated me. Matteo had my juice box sopping wet and still dripping like a snow cone, I felt like I was about to drown in my own juices.

"Who make you sick, Sommer? Hmm? I make you sick? You really want me to just throw this dick deep in yo' muthafuckin' guts don't you?"

Matteo let me know with every pump he was in control; the only thing I could do was blink and respond. I was pissed, but damn if that shit didn't feel good. I felt every last stroke, every last vein on him, every last throb as his dick matched the beat deep down in my pussy. "Mmm... no, baby... you don't make me sick."

He licked the side of my face, biting my neck as I came for the second time; still frozen in place. Grabbing my chin, he rubbed his tongue across my lips. I flicked my tongue against his before he inhaled my face for the umpteenth time. "Marry me, Dr. Park. You ain't even gotta take my last name, I just need you in my life—"

"Yes, Matteo...yes...whatever you say, the answer is yes."

"I love you, Sommer. I'm your family. You ain't never gonna be alone again. You got me, and we got us."

"And the baby?"

"And the baby."

"OUR baby, Matteo. If anybody else pregnant—"

"WE a family, baby," he grabbed my waist, and we switched positions so I was on top. "I'll take care of that for you, baby."

I loved it when he called me his baby; wrapped up in his arms I felt safe and protected. Matteo gave me love, he gave me peace, he was the harmony in my soul. I wrapped my hand around his neck and applied pressure while I bounced up and down on his dick. "She good to you, Matteo?"

"Damn, baby, this pussy good as fuck," he moaned, trying to control his nut. "You 'bout to make me cum—"

"Cum for me—mmm… there he go," I whispered at the same time his seed spilled inside me in spurts. "There he go. That's all me, Matteo Marino. Don't you forget it."

"Never."

I laid on his chest and listened to his heartbeat beginning to slow down and return to normal. We were in total and complete sync with one another, and it made my heart full. I couldn't believe he asked me to marry him, and I shocked myself even more when I said yes. I loved Matteo, but we still had some things to work out before I could walk down an aisle and give myself to him for the rest of my life.

"Aye, I know y'all ain't fucking in my guestroom!" Reno yelled through the oak door. "One of y'all better get up and wash them damn sheets!"

"Aye, fuck you, nigga!"

"Betta had brought yo' ass over here. I was about to slide if you would've waited 'til tomorrow. Nutted all on ya son's forehead too!" he shuffled away from the door, chuckling to himself.

"Slide in my girl's room and I'ma slide you in a quick prayer to let God know you on ya way, bruh!" he yelled back. "You was gonna give my brother some pussy?" Matteo questioned playfully, pulling my hair.

"Naw." I snickered at both Marino brothers, because they were definitely some comedians. "Reno was a gentleman the entire time. Now if Luca was here—"

"I'ma beat yo' ass," he leaned in, biting my bottom lip before he took another kiss. "You know my trigger finger stay on go mode. Get that man shot, that's what you do."

"You not gonna shoot your brother over me, stop it." I snickered, pecking the tip of his nose.

"Lay on my chest again, I like that." Resting my head on his heart, I let him continue to absently run his fingers through my hair. "Why you keep saying you hate me?"

"If I like you… I mean, seriously see myself with you for the long term… nine times outta ten, you drive me crazy. Out of the handful of people I've been with in the past, you the only one who has the power to either make my entire day or irritate my entire soul."

"Damn, baby. That's sweet, but it's kinda fucked up."

"Why you say that?"

"You know how I feel about you?"

"Yeah. You love me."

"I more than love you, Sommer."
Matteo's fingertips danced up and down my
spine as he spoke. "I wanna make you
happy. The kind of happy that when you lay
in the bed next to me at night, you say to
yourself, 'Wow. Who even knew this was
possible?' You ever been that kind of happy,
baby?"

"No." I yawned softly. His deep timbre
was my lullaby rocking me and our baby to
sleep.

"I can't wait until we get married. I
wanna cuddle with you, tickle you until you
get mad, play hide-and-seek just so I can
scare the shit outta you…"

"Go to sleep." I rolled over and covered
his mouth so he'd shut up.

"You can ignore me all you want, I'm
still gonna marry you." In a short time I
found the man who put a smile on my face
and love in my soul. Matteo was the reason I

went to sleep with a smile on my face every night.

Matteo

Reno's house wasn't as comfortable as mine, but Sommer was only here for the night, so I put up with it for the time being. Not to mention, it was convenient for me and Reno to continue our conversation from last night. I had to know what the connection was between David and my parents, and although he couldn't remember exact details from that fateful day, he was the key.

Checking my phone after I left the house on 104th, I saw I had a text from Xander. Tapping the screen twice to open the message, I wasn't shocked to see Keedra was pregnant. The question was, who was she pregnant by? Was it mine? Or was it Luca's? I didn't want to deprive the next man of his seed, but Keedra couldn't go full term with this baby if it was mine, according to Sommer.

The more fucked up part was I cheated on a woman I claimed to love with a woman I know for a fact I didn't. If Keedra WAS pregnant by me, I knew her jealous nature all too well. She'd make it her business to come to my house whenever she felt like it to rub what we did in Sommer's face and get her ass kicked every time. As much as I enjoyed seeing Keedra's face smashed against the concrete… nah. We had to get this thing out in the open, I wasn't going to subject Sommer to that especially with her being pregnant with a baby I knew without a doubt belonged to me.

"Hey you," Sommer appeared from out the bathroom taking care of her hygiene. "You hungry?"

"Mmhmm."

"What you want to eat, love?"

"Kinda wanna spread vanilla icing on your pussy, add sprinkles, and eat it like a cupcake." I reached out and pulled her on the bed with me. "What you eating?"

"Reno made me some food, so I'ma eat that," she straddled my waist, sitting her plump booty in my lap while she rubbed my beard. "Lemme braid this."

"You know how to braid?"

"No."

"You good, then." I smacked her ass, scraping her panty clad pussy back and forth across my lower half. "Lemme eat this."

"You know how?"

"Hell yeah."

"You good then," she grinned smugly, sliding her hands down the sides of her panties to take them off. I helped her out, ripping the thin material out of my way. With one move, I had her on the bed, booty cheeks hiked in the air while I feasted on her pearl. "Matteooo—mmm, get full baby."

"Mmhmm—gimme some juice to go with my food."

"AAAHHH MATTEO! SHIT!" I loved making her scream, that pussy right there loved me.

"That should get you through the day." I kissed her caramel colored, peach shaped lower lips before smoothing a hand from her titties to her pussy. "Yo' lil stomach firm. Why didn't I notice that while we was overseas?"

"Because you were more focused on my kewchie," she mumbled while I lowered her bottom half against the cool sheets. "I noticed it, and that's why I took the pregnancy test."

"I wish you would've told me first. I wanted to be there and wait with you." I loved pulling her hair back, gripping her thick strands in my fist.

"Mentally I had a lot to sort out before I took that test. I'm sorry baby, I really wanted to be alone at the time."

"But you called my brother though?"

"I was mad at you. What's wrong you don't want me calling your brother?"

"So—you know what. We'll talk about it when we get home. Where your bag?"

"I ain't going home." She scrunched her face up at me before swinging her feet over the edge of the bed, hopping down and heading for the door.

"What you mean 'you ain't going home'?"

"Just what I said. Thanks for the dick, but we still got problems."

"We still got problems? What you mean we still got problems?" I snapped. "You said yes to my proposal and you carrying my baby, so what problems we got?"

"Matteo, if you don't know, it's not my job to tell you." She opened the door and walked out of Reno's spare bedroom, slamming it behind her.

Sommer said I was the one who had the power to either make her day or irritate the fuck outta her. Judging by the way she was moving, it was definitely the other way around. I'd be here for as long as it took for her to understand I wasn't leaving Reno's without her.

Keedra

"Bitch, I swear to God—" Nezz began, unbuttoning his pants.

"It's our secret as long as you ain't recording," I cooed, inching closer to his massive tool. "I'm not telling him, so if he finds out—"

Nezz gripped the back of my head, forcing me to go down on him. Tears rushed to my eyes, and I almost choked until I relaxed my throat when he slipped past my gag reflex.

"Mmm… make it sloppy for me, bitch." I slurped and gagged on his thick, chocolate manhood until he erupted stickiness down my throat. Whatever Nezz wanted, I was all in as long as Matteo didn't find out I wasn't pregnant.

Matteo was so pressed about whether or not I was with child, I figured it had something to do with his precious Sommer. Nezz bandaged my hand up once he left; Matteo's knife went through clean and came out the other end. All because of *that* bitch. Naw, I wasn't pregnant, but I'd happily be the reason she left his ass. Even if we didn't get back together, he didn't deserve to be happy, nor did she.

"That was good. Now you only owe me twelve more of those before your debt is paid." Nezz got a lil' chick he knew to doctor the pregnancy test and switched it with the one Xander had to send to Matteo, tossing mine in the trash. From what he told me, he worked with one of Matteo's associates who got him the interview with Luca. He worked with Luca on some special project that was top secret, and Luca sent him to the house where I was being held. They talked all that shit about them being 'the Marino boys', yet it was only a matter of time before Nezz slit both of their throats. Hopefully, it'd be after Matteo wrote his will and included me in it. The Marino name alone was worth millions of dollars that was tied up in stocks, investments, real estate, and cash.

"Did Matteo say I could leave yet?" After all, I was kidnapped while I was still in my pajamas, which meant I was sitting on a cold, steel chair dressed in a silk robe with a red Chantilly lace teddy underneath. I stayed ready for whatever might happen, whenever it happened, even if it was at my mama house. Her front porch was dark, almost pitch black. She'd never know if I was out there getting fucked underneath the steps.

"Naw." He shoved the red face towel in my mouth, which served as a temporary gag. "Sit tight until I give the word."

Watching his huge silhouette lumber out of the dimly lit room, I waited until he was completely out of my peripheral vision before my head dropped in shame. I didn't like what I did, but it wasn't too much else I could do. My reputation preceded me wherever I went, and no matter how hard I tried to get away from it, whenever someone said 'Keedra', the word 'hoe' always came up. After a while, I just said fuck it and embraced it. If I was gonna be labeled as a hoe, I'd be the best lil' hoe Milwaukee had to offer.

How long was I supposed to stay here, wherever 'here' was though? I had stuff to do, like go watch Matteo. My mama wasn't looking for me? What time was it? I dozed off for a few minutes about an hour ago, but I needed a bath and to be back in my own bed so I could come up with a better plot. Matteo really thought he was doing something. I ain't have time for that 'we done' shit. "We done when I say we done," I whispered softly. "And according to me, we ain't done."

I rubbed my swollen, throbbing palm; my fingers looked like Vienna sausages each time I tried making a fist. I needed to be at somebody's urgent care, but I wanted to see my 'baby daddy's' face once more before I did. He needed to see the pain he inflicted on me, the mother of his 'first child'. Giggling to myself, I got as comfortable as I could in the chair and waited for Nezz to come untie my ankles so I could get *my* husband back, and *we* could be a family.

Luca

"Who pregnant?"

"Yo' girl. Keedra." Matteo giggled in my ear, but I didn't find nothing funny.

"How you know it ain't yours? She lived in the house with you!" I grunted, gripping my phone a little tighter.

Matteo stopped laughing, his voice dropping a half octave. "I ain't nut in Keedra."

"Me either." *Wait, did I?* That whole Pornhub thing happened a few months ago; I barely remembered what happened that night. "What she gonna do?"

"Fuck am I supposed to know? Keedra can swallow a dog's dick for all I care, she ain't my responsibility. Aye, on some real shit though, why you go do the exact opposite of what I told you to do? You think

I need to be associated with Sleazo and everything that comes with that?"

"Matteo, I ain't know he had nothing to do with what me and David had going on. He introduced us and said that was it."

"That's the thing, Luca; that ain't it. You know them diamonds you buying off of him?"

"Yeah."

"Blood diamonds. Know what else he smuggling in with those diamonds?"

"What? Dope?"

"Kids, man. They kidnapping kids from other countries and bringing them out here. You being associated with him associates us with that shit."

"Kids?"

"I'm 'bout to be a father soon. I ain't trying—"

"So Keedra baby is yours then, huh?" I cackled in his ear.

"Sommer baby is mine."

"Sommer?" Now I was mad all over again. How my brother get a baby before me? "Oh, uhhh...congrats, man."

"Luca, lemme ask you something. You knew Sommer was at Potawatomie for a few weeks, right?"

"Yeah."

"All that time she was there, did she ever—"

"Did she ever what?"

"Did she ever say anything to you about anything?"

"Why you ask me that, Matteo?"

"Nothing. I'm tripping. Look, I'm at Reno's crib for a while, so if you can't get me at the house, come out here."

"We making the drops at Reno's spot now?" I tried to change the subject, but my mind was still on Matteo asking me about Sommer. She must've said something to him about me, which meant she was thinking about me as much as I was thinking about her.

"Nah, drops still go to the other house. Aye, I got a call coming in that I gotta take. I'll get up with you later, aight?" Matteo hurriedly clicked over to the other line, and I hung up, intrigued.

Matteo was always telling me to respect his relationship, but from what I could tell, his relationship was more focused on respecting me. Why else would he ask me if Sommer let a real G hit? Not saying my brother wasn't out here knocking these women down, but deep down, Sommer knew which one of the Marino boys would give her that work. Oouu—and now with her being pregnant, I knew that pussy was super wet-wet. I had to figure out a way to get close to her so I could find out.

Reno was ringing my phone for some odd reason; I was just about to see if Ina missed her period yet. "What?"

"You doing stupid shit is fucking up my end of the business, that's what."

"What is you talking about, Reno?"

"I got pedophiles calling me because they heard you was in business with Sleazo. Fix this shit, Luca. I'd hate to have to body yo' stupid ass for putting money before common fucking sense!" he spat in my ear before hanging up. My phone beeped with a text message from Reno. I opened it to see what he felt the need to say as if we hadn't just got off the phone:

Reno: *FIX THIS SHIT, LUCA!*

Guess I gotta fix this shit. I sighed to myself, running my hand over my head before getting out of bed. I had to take a shower and get out here in the streets. Reno was now up to deadlifting 450lbs, knew where I lived, and had the alarm code. *How both of 'em mad at me?* I thought, shaking my head before turning on the water in the shower stall.

Reno

Whatever Luca and Matteo had going on between them was between them, but when I started getting calls from anybody looking for kids, that shit was a no go. We didn't even sell dope to kids when we were younger; I damn sure wasn't about to be doing no shit like that. Plus, I had a niece or nephew coming soon, and if a muthafucka touched a hair on his or her head, looked at them wrong, or made them cry… Matteo wouldn't have to handle that because I would.

I had plans on being uncle of the year; I loved kids. Kids that weren't mine though… I could spoil the hell out of them and give 'em back. Sommer and Matteo was gonna hate me, but oh well. Knowing my brother, that kid was gonna be spoiled anyway, whether Sommer liked it or not. I hoped it was a girl. Before Sommer, we didn't have any females in the family after Ma, and Pop gave her everything she thought she might've wanted.

Pop was a street legend. He didn't dabble in dope or anything, he just worked hard at his job. They lived in our old neighborhood for years, so everybody knew who he was. I heard whispers that he used to smuggle in that good dope from overseas, but we were so young when he died that we weren't privy to what he had going on for real.

My aunt had a nice house on the edge of the city that she claimed her husband worked hard at Miller Brewing Company for years, and they saved their money. Bullshit, she stole that money from us when my mother died. My grandma told me the whole story before she died. Long story short, Pop put everything in his sister's name in case anything happened to him or Moms, and she kept the money for her own kids when they died. We hated her when we were younger, but now that she comes to us begging for money every couple of months, it was funny. I'd tell her to call Luca, he told her to call Matteo, and Matteo told her to go fuck herself. Didn't stop her from begging though.

After talking to my brother last night, bits and pieces of that day all those years ago were coming back to me. I still couldn't remember who the men were in the room, but I was starting to recall the conversation I walked in on. Pop was saying something to one of the men about respect, and someone else was in the midst of speaking up when... everything else became blurry again.

The fact this David person knew enough about us to disrespect my mother by insinuating she knew Sleazo... that had me heated. I was surprised Matteo didn't kill his ass, but knowing my brother, David was still alive because there were too many witnesses at the casino. My brother was known for putting in work, and it wasn't nothing nice.

They claimed I was the angry one, but nah. Matteo's temper would scare the shit out of the devil himself. I'd seen him torture men without blinking an eye and shoot up blocks because one nigga might've shorted him a dollar by accident. This one time, I walked up on him gutting a man in an alley in broad daylight. He turned around with intestines on his hands talking 'bout, *what you want, Reno?* What I didn't want was to see that shit. David didn't know what he started when he alluded he was my brother's father. Matteo was the type that would creep in your window in the middle of the day, slit your throat, then show up at your funeral knowing he had your blood on his hands to admire his work.

If he needed some help with that whole David thing though, I was all in. I don't be in the same circles as my brothers for a reason, and that's because I was the one who didn't ask questions. Anybody fucking with my family got dealt with, period. My brothers had been there for me growing up, now it was my responsibility to be there for them as men. Matteo and Luca had that whole sibling rivalry thing going on, and that was between them. More Luca than Matteo, but that's usually how it goes. Rarely did it go further than that, but Luca had been on some real petty bullshit lately. I didn't know what they had going on; but knowing them, they'd get over it.

Meanwhile, I had somebody I was interested in, and we were taking it slow because she was currently with somebody. I loved her vibe though; she was cool, laid back, and low key. I needed that type of woman to calm the beast who lived in my head. My rage used to get to the point where it was unbearable. Hearing from her soothed me, feeling her relaxed me. Yeah, she stayed with her guy, but that was coming to an end soon. Especially since she was carrying my baby; I didn't want my son coming into the world thinking another man was his father.

I went to every doctor's appointment, and hearing his heartbeat for the first time was it for me. Matteo knew I was trying to get out of the business, but I never told him why. I appreciated that about my brother; he never forced me to go into detail about the moves I made. Luca, on the other hand, hadn't put nothing in the money pot in a while, yet he felt like he had an equal say on everything we invested in. Most of the time we ignored him.

Either way, I needed both of my brothers' full attention in the event my girl's boyfriend decided he wanted to pull up on me over her. I could handle my own, but knowing who her guy was... Matteo and Luca might need to step in.

Sommer

"Hey, brother-in-law." Reno paused to clear his throat, almost like I was interrupting him while he was in deep thought as I plopped down at the kitchen table. "Where my food?"

"On the stove. Plates in the cabinet and spoons in the first drawer closest to the sink."

"Wow, Reno. You ain't gonna fix my plate?" I pouted, pushing my chair back and heading toward the stove. "That's how you do the mother of your first niece or nephew?"

"Ain't nothing wrong with your hands, you can fix your own food. Matteo ain't 'bout to come down here and accuse me of—" He stopped suddenly. From the look on his face, I could pretty much figure out what his next words would be.

"Accuse us of having sex?"

"I ain't never accused you of fucking Reno. Luca, maybe, but Reno, naw." Matteo walked in the kitchen with his shirt off, chest rippling, and looking like a black Adonis. If Reno wasn't standing at the counter making waffles, I would've hopped up on the quartz island in the middle of the chef's kitchen and spread my legs wide enough for him to finish his breakfast.

"You think I fucked your brother, Matteo Constantine Marino?" I slid a small knife from the butcher's block on the countertop and held it against his right nipple. When I saw the twinkle in his eye as a smile spread across his face, I knew he liked crazy stuff like that.

"And she know ya full name, big bro? Yeah, wife her up." Reno instigated, flipping waffles out the waffle maker.

"I didn't say you did." Matteo ignored his brother, grabbing a strawberry from the bowl on the table and taking a bite as I sat on the stool reminiscing about our sounds of lovemaking from last night. "What I said was maybe. You don't listen, do you?" he curled his tongue around the juicy fruit, rivers of nectar wetting his lips.

"I do listen. Keep playing with me like I'm not a doctor who know where all your vital organs are." I was still trying to scare him, pressing the pointed tip harder against his skin.

"Mmm... stab me, Sommer." Matteo moved closer to the knife, smiling the whole time. "When you done, I'ma stab the fuck outta you next," my love murmured in my ear, licking his lips before flicking his tongue across my mouth.

"You just gonna stab my brother in front of me, huh?" Reno spoke up from his spot near the sink. "After I was nice enough to let you stay at my house?"

"Sommer ain't doing shit with that lil' knife. Won't even puncture my skin, much less a damn lung." Matteo cackled crazily in my face.

"Fix my food, Matteo Marino." I slammed the knife on the counter and sat back down at the table. "I want some everything."

"You want some dick too? I gotchu once you finish this food," Matteo replied nonchalantly, grabbing a plate from the cabinet.

"Nah, you can keep that lil' peen in your pants. I'm cool with bacon, sausage, eggs, hash browns, and them buttermilk biscuits." I folded my fingers on the table in front of me, dangling my feet while waiting for my plate.

"Just a big ass kid, man." Matteo snickered, shaking his head while piling my plate with food. "This lil' peen got you pregnant though, didn't it."

"Anybody can nut, it don't take that much."

"Anybody can't have your eyes rolled in the back of yo' head while you shuddering that cum out, can they?" he kissed my neck, sending chills through my body. "That takes skills, mama."

"Whatever, Matteo. We starving."

"Eat this while I fix you some waffles." Matteo placed a plate full of food in front of me and I didn't care about Reno watching me, I dug into my meal. My teeth sank into the fluffy biscuits first, I closed my eyes and took a deep breath to savor the flavors and Matteo wiped the butter from the corner of my lip with his fingertip. "Look at yo' lil' hungry butt making a mess already."

"Mmm, baby, why you ain't tell me Reno can cook?" I mumbled, dropping biscuit crumbs down the front of my shirt.

"Oh, yeah, Reno is the black Bobby Flay. Not only do he have his hand in the streets, he's also trained at Lé Cordón Bleu for a year," Matteo quipped, forking two Belgian waffles onto another plate for me.

"For real?"

"Hell naw, Reno used to play in the food when we was kids. Give this man some flour, sugar, milk, and an egg and he'll give you a cake fresh out the bakery. He made this frosting one time with some brown sugar, cinnamon, and egg whites that tasted like something from one of these five star restaurants. If it wasn't for lil' bro though, we would've starved a few nights."

"Where was your mother?"

"Aye, you like crêpes?" Reno interrupted from the sink where he'd gotten started on the dishes. They say cleanliness is next to godliness, and that description fit him to a T. "I got a recipe for strawberry and cream cheese stuffed crêpes with a berry infused syrup drizzled on top that'll put you to sleep."

"I'll put her to sleep, we don't need your help." Matteo spoke up. "Eat your food, mama." Scooping a forkful of eggs and hash browns, he held the food to my mouth and encouraged me to eat. Matteo fed me both plates while I sat patiently at the table and got full.

"You spoiling that girl already." Reno dried the last dish and stuck it in the cabinet before pulling up a stool to the island. "She ain't even had that baby yet, and you over there feeding her."

"Not only is she carrying my sole heir, but she said yes. Why wouldn't I spoil her?"

he responded, dabbing the corners of my mouth with a napkin. "This my baby."

As happy as I wanted to be for my pregnancy and upcoming motherhood, I couldn't, knowing what I'd left at the house. That sonogram. That sonogram would forever haunt me until I knew for sure it wasn't his. And if it was, he'd never see it. "Find out about that other baby, then we'll talk." I pushed the chair back from the table and started toward the steps. Matteo grabbed my wrist, stopping me dead in my tracks.

"I told you I ain't got but one baby. Even if half of Milwaukee said I got them pregnant, I ain't gonna never give a fuck about no other kids, Sommer. You who I want. You who I need. You who I—"

"Say it, bro!" Reno yelled, watching our love story unfold in the suburbs.

Grabbing my chin, he pulled my face so close to his we were sharing air. "You who I love. I'm at my brother's house with you because of you. If you wanna talk, we can talk. If you wanna be mad, be mad. Whatever it is, I'm here. I'm at your beck and call. I ain't leaving you here or nowhere else, so when you wanna come home, we going together. You understand me, Sommer?"

"Yes," I whispered. What else could I say? When Matteo Marino talked to me like that, it was only one thing my mind screamed for me to do. "You uhmm… you wanna go upstairs and talk?"

"Yeah, we can talk." Matteo slapped my ass with a devilish look in his eye, letting go of my wrist while gripping a handful of my booty cheek. "Let's have some angry conversation. I'm 'bout to talk to that pussy… I mean, yeah, let's come to some sort of resolution. We can't keep going back and forth like this."

"I'm 'bout to go back and forth, up and down, side to side… wait. You right, we need to be adults about this."

"Gon' hit that shit, bro!" Reno wasn't shit; he knew what was about to go down. "Take y'all ass home after this though!"

Matteo bit down hard on my booty cheek as he climbed the steps behind me, and I still felt the imprint of his teeth. With one move, he swooped my little self over his shoulder, carrying me the rest of the way. "Boy, I'll go soak up the sheets on your bed if I wanted to!" I yelled out from the top of the steps. "Go home? I just lost my sister and I got a step kid, I'm comfortable! You heard him, bae? He said for us to go home!" I smirked loud enough for Reno to hear as Matteo carried me down the hall. Dipping quickly inside the bedroom right next to my brother-in-law's, he kicked the door shut while I rubbed on his hard chest.

"You must not be mad at me no more." Matteo pulled closer and nuzzled his face in the crook of my neck.

"I might be willing to listen to what you have to say."

"We can be adults later. Right now, we 'bout to be some savages. Is that ok with you, pretty gurl?"

"I'm in love with a savage, so we can do that."

Laying me on the bed, Matteo slowly removed what little clothes I had on piece by piece. "After today, I don't want you to ever doubt my love for you again. I promised you it was me and you against the world, and that's what I meant," he murmured while his fingers danced provocatively over my skin.

"I'm not mad at you anymore, Matteo," I whispered, hissing lowly when he entered me.

"I know you ain't. You wasn't mad at me anyway, you just called yo'self putting that pretty foot of yours down."

"From this point on, you are MINE Matteo Marino. You hear me?" I moaned, locking my legs around his waist.

"I been yours and you been mine. But if you wanna play you making the plays, I'm good with that." He raised my leg and tucked it in the crook of his arm before sliding sideways so he could plunge deeper inside my pussy.

"Matteo—"

"I wanna hear your heart beat in my ear every night. I carry you here. You live right here, Sommer." He took my hand and placed it over his chest. "I can't wait to make you my wife."

"I can't wait to be your wife, Matteo." I verbalized just above a whisper. Shannie popped in my head; suddenly I remembered

I had no one to invite to my wedding and no one to share that moment with. No one to be my maid of honor and no mother to help me pick out my dress. No sister to kiss my head and tell me how beautiful I looked in my dress, no sister to playfully chastise about when she'd find a husband. Torrie and Lana were already married, and while they'd always stepped in and played the role of my sisters, it was different when there was a person who, at one time, I shared a face with.

"What's wrong, bae? Am I hurting you?" Matteo's voice was worried in my ear. My eyes were full as the wetness slid slowly down my face.

"No, baby." I sniffed quietly. "I'm ok."

"Love, you not ok," he wiped my tears with the crook of his finger. "Baby—"

"She's gone, Matteo. My sister is gone. Who do…" I wept, trying to control the flood of sadness as it washed over my soul leaving me drenched in sorrow. "Who do I share this moment in my life with?"

"Me, baby. Share it with me." Matteo consoled, wiping my face. "We're family. You know I got you."

"I know, but—"

"Listen," he shifted and laid next to me. "I don't need you stressed out, so I took care of her arrangements. She's gonna be buried near my parents on our family plot. What else do you need for me to do, love?"

"I—baby, I don't know. I don't know how these things go. I never had to bury anyone," I confessed. "With the baby, an engagement, my parents, this thing with you... I haven't had a chance to grieve my sister."

"Take the thing with me off your plate, we good." He tucked a hair behind my ear and spoke quietly. "I don't make empty promises. Daddy gonna take care of that whole sonogram thing for us. I need to know too."

"No you don't."

"Yes I do. If I tell you it's all about us, it's all about us. Fuck a baby," he chuckled, eyes twinkling.

"How did I get so lucky to have you?" I slid closer to him and tucked under his solid frame where I felt safe.

"Thank your brother-in-law for sending me to kidnap you. If Luca hadn't—"

"Luca sent you to kidnap me?" I sat up, shocked. This was the first time I was hearing this story. "For what?"

"Yeah. He claimed you were Shannie, and at the time we didn't know about her having a twin."

Luca really was crazy. His brothers kept saying he was, I just didn't believe them Now I'm convinced. "Matteo?"

"Sommer."

"Thank you for making my sister's funeral arrangements. I don't know the first thing about none of that."

"I know, sweetie. You just need to rest and—" we were interrupted by a knock on the door. "What's going on, Reno?"

"Matteo, we got a problem. I know you and wife in there making up, but it's important."

"Go ahead, love. I'll be ok." I encouraged, knowing how he was. "If you have to go—"

"I'm not leaving this house without you knowing, calm down," Matteo soothed. When he kissed my head, his lips anywhere on my body had me blushing; I liked it when he did that. "Reno! What's so important that I can't spend time with my wife?"

"It's Luca."

Matteo took a deep breath in and shook his head, opening the door. "What this idiot got going on now?" he mumbled lowly, no doubt hoping I couldn't hear him.

"You ever heard of a nigga named Nezz?" Reno questioned seriously as him and his brother started heading down the steps.

Matteo

Nodding at the concierge in Luca's
building, I calmly walked over and pushed
the button on the elevator for the eighteenth
floor. As the elevator settled quietly behind
the metal doors in front of me, I took a
moment to check my overall appearance, not
wanting to give off the look as if I didn't
belong. After I left Reno's home, I stopped
off at my spot and changed clothes so I'd fit
in with the residents in Luca's building.
Therefore no one would suspect anything in
case something went down between me and
my brother.

The ride to Luca's floor was brief.
Stepping off and heading to his condo, I
nodded at an older lady and her husband
who nodded approvingly in my direction
once her husband turned his head. She had a
look in her eyes that said she'd ask me to

'help' her take her teeth out so she could rape me with her mouth.

Tapping in my code on the keypad outside of Luca's door, I eased in quietly and shut the door behind me. Strolling calmly across the expensive rugs covering the floor, I pulled the pistol from the waistband of my tailored pants and took the safety off. "Ooouuu, Luca," a woman's voice moaned sultrily from his bedroom. "Wait... slow down... put the tip in. You know I can't take the whole thing..."

"Either fuck it or suck it, Sakina. You know how I like my pus..."

I walked in his bedroom with my pistol trained on both of them. "She gonna suck it. Ain't that what they always do, lil' bro?" I laughed disrespectfully at Sakina as she rushed to cover herself up.

"To what do I owe this pleasure?" Luca uttered calmly, folding his hands behind his head while leaning back on the pillows of his Cali king. "The great Matteo Marino blessing me with his presence! Thought you didn't come to the Mil, bro."

"Depends on the occasion. Thought about sending somebody, but then changed my mind and decided to handle it myself," I responded nonchalantly. "What happened to Ina?"

"She left." Luca's mood changed, but I got the feeling he wasn't about to go into detail about why.

"On her own, or you motivated her to do so?"

"On her own! Matteo, you think I'm gonna do something to the mother of my first child?"

"Where she go?"

The look on his face became more pronounced, he definitely had something to do with it. I just didn't know what. "She didn't say."

I knew if I kept asking questions, Luca was gonna start lying and I wasn't in the mood. "Tell me about Nezz, lil' bro."

"Nezz?" Luca feigned surprised, even raised his eyebrow at me. "The new connect, Nezz?"

"Matteo, if you just lemme grab my clothes, I promise—" Sakina leaned over the side of the bed and tried to plead her case.

"Bitch, my brother seen pussy before, stop trying to cover up! He 'married' now." Luca air quoted, his tone laced with venom.

"Please, Matteo," Sakina begged, ignoring the man whose bed she was just getting fucked in. "I promise—"

"Shoot her!" Luca yelled out, exasperated. "These hoes ain't loyal! I hate that shit!"

I muffed Sakina's head backward as my brother caught her around the neck and began choking her out. "What the fuck wrong with you, man!"

"Sicka these bitches!" Luca roared with a crazed look in his eye while Sakina clawed at his hand trying to loosen his grip. "I treat these hoes like royalty, yet she in here staring at you like she wanna suck your dick! She in here begging YOU for some fucking mercy! Beg me, bitch! BEG FOR YO' FUCKIN' LIFE!"

I grabbed the pistol and pulled the trigger, shooting a hole in the wall behind him to snap out of his daze. "Luca, let that girl go! Damn, you been wildin' out lately! What the fuck is wrong with you!"

Luca finally snapped out of his daze and let Sakina go, dropping her to the floor coughing and taking deep breaths to try and get air back in her lungs. "Get out of here, bitch!" He tossed a few twenties in her direction, watching her intently snatch her clothes from the bedroom floor.

"Stay the fuck away from me, Luca! This the last time you put hands on me, muthafucka!"

I pulled her to the side before she stormed out of the apartment. Per usual, I had to do some damage control before this wild nigga got us locked up. "Aye, get cleaned up before you go, aight?" I peeled a few hundreds off the knot in my pocket.

"Thank you, Matteo. Your brother been tripping lately, you need to do something about that," she gritted lowly, sliding her clothes on before leaving without another word.

I focused my gaze back on my brother, who was sitting in his bed watching me. "Let's see, you a diamond dealer selling blood diamonds, a human trafficker, woman beater, and trying to get me killed because I'm not babysitting yo' old ass no more. Did I forget anything?"

"Who said I was trying to kill you, Matteo? You my brother, why would I do that?" Luca tried to come off as innocent, yet I saw when his hand slid under the pillow.

"Luca, don't make me shoot you." I warned, pistol aimed at his head. "I love you enough to be the one to put you out of your misery just so another nigga ain't going around bragging about it."

"I'm not miserable, Matteo." Luca pulled a cigar from underneath the pillow along with a lighter. Flipping the pillows over so I could see he didn't have anything else underneath, he stood up naked with his hands in the air and a Montecristo in his mouth.

"Stand over there by the window." I motioned, still not sure of what was going on with him. "If you ain't miserable, why is Nezz trying to kill me? As a matter of fact, why is Nezz trying to kill US?"

"Us? Kill? Matteo, what you talking about?" He leaned comfortably against the window, ass smashed against the glass while he lit up. "Yeah, I know Nezz ain't the connect. Yeah, I sent him to fuck with you. So what."

"Luca, I'm not 'bout to be going back and forth with you. What's the issue, cause we not 'bout to keep playing 'guess who'."

Luca took a long pull off the cigar, dumping ashes on the floor while he debated whether or not he was gonna talk. "Other than you completely ignoring our bond—"

"That's the same shit Keedra was talking," I cackled, Luca was starting to sound like a bitch. "Try again."

"Matteo, you been giving us guidance all these years, now all of a sudden you ain't. What we supposed to do?" he snapped. "How you go from the king of Milwaukee to a wife and kids? All over a bitch who got you spending all our money—"

"First of all, ain't no 'our money'!" I snapped, punching the wall. The more he talked the madder I got. "Second, she got her own damn money! If you watched Ma and Pop, you'd know a real one when you met her! Sommer a whole ass doctor out here, hell a few of YO' bitches probably on her waiting list! You worried about what I'm doing!"

"Fuck her, Matteo! FUCK HER! Shoot that bitch, get yo' fucking head back in the game and let's get this money!" Luca roared back.

I punched Luca's ass before I knew it, next minute we were tussling on the floor, him still naked. "Let me go Matteo! LET ME GO!"

"Listen to me cause I'm only gonna say this one time," I growled, pinning him on the bed with a hand around his neck. He was still naked, so I stood on his right side. "Let something happen to Sommer and I'm bodying you, Luca. I'm done playing these games with you. Grow the fuck up, my nigga!"

"Everybody loves Matteo! Keedra loves Matteo. Sommer loves Matteo… EVERYBODY FUCKIN' LOVES MATTEO!"

"Luca—"

"No matter how much we fuck up, you always been there to fix it. When I broke that window when we was kids, YOU took the blame! When Renato shot Pop in the head, YOU told him everything was gonna be ok! When Ma started spiraling out of control, and we went days without so much as a sandwich, YOU went to the corner store and stole us some powdered doughnuts!"

"We was kids! I ain't know what I was doing no more than you did!"

"As many women out here in the streets as we tag teamed, you never gave a fuck about none of 'em!" I loosened my grip on his neck as Luca continued. "Hell, all three of us hit Keedra that one night two years ago."

"Damn, you know I forgot about that?" I thought back to that night after I killed Keedra's friend, Maritza. We all agreed she needed something to keep her in line. Make her not forget who she was crossing so she'd never bring her friends around us again. For some reason, she still stayed, even after that. Clout chasing is a hell of a drug.

"Now you got a girl you won't share. Now you 'in love'," he air quoted. "Now you ain't your brother's keeper. That's bullshit, Matteo!"

I released my grip and sat on the edge of the bed next to him. "Luca, if I wasn't my brother's keeper, yo' ass would be dead. Which brings me back to this nigga Nezz—"

"I'll take care of Nezz, Matteo. Thanks for telling me he was on some other shit. What about this nigga David, though?" Luca suddenly changed the subject. "Does Reno remember anything?"

"Nah. He say it was so long ago he barely remembers." I made a mental note not to show any of my usual tells around my brother. I didn't like him shushing me like I was one of these lil' niggas on the block. This wasn't about Sommer, it couldn't be. But what was it about?

"Well, we should meet up when he does remember. Take care of David as soon as we know something, right, Matteo?"

"Yeah, we can do that. Speaking of which, aye, come walk me out. I just remembered I had to go take care of this little situation at the house." I waited and let him go first. My street intuition told me not to trust my own brother, and that bothered me.

"See you at the drop off spot later, I got something to contribute." Luca's tone changed again. He was suddenly cheerful as if he didn't try to kill that girl five minutes ago.

"Aight see you, lil' bro." We exchanged goodbyes as he smiled brightly before closing the door. I pulled out my phone and called Reno. "Aye, do me a favor."

"What you need, Matteo?"

"First and foremost, keep this conversation between me and you. Second, pick up everything at the spot and dump it in that one place." I spoke in code, but Reno knew exactly what I meant. He needed to empty the vault at the trap mansion and deposit the money in our Cayman accounts.

"Aight. I take it you saw Luca?"

"We'll discuss that when I get back."

"Aight. See you in a bit." Reno hurriedly ended our call. I stopped at Luca's cars, all parked in a line in his assigned parking spot and poked a hole in one tire on all three cars. Hopefully, the thoughts in my mind about him weren't true. Hopefully, I was being paranoid. But I noticed when I mentioned Nezz trying to kill both of us was when our conversation changed. Nezz wasn't supposed to be trying to kill Luca. He was supposed to kill ME.

Luca

After Matteo left, I finished my cigar before hopping in the shower. David had been blowing my phone up since we left him in the hotel, and I wasn't in the mood to hear nothing he had to say. This man said he was Matteo's father and insinuated my mother wasn't faithful to Pops. He knew Matteo was my brother… all this time, he'd been using me to get to him. I ain't like that shit.

"What you want?" I decided to see what he had to say, wasn't like Matteo was gonna be around for much longer in the first place.

"I'm not understanding what the issue is." David's thick English accent seemed to be confused. "How do you not see the resemblance between me and your brother?"

Matteo looked like a slightly darker version of my father. He didn't look… like… "That wasn't the time or place for you to have that conversation with him, whether you are or aren't. What did you think he was gonna do?"

"Regardless, have your brother call me so he and I can talk man to man. He doesn't need to be in this small town running drugs when he's the heir to—"

"To what?"

"Have your brother call me. Goodbye, Luca Marino." David abruptly ended the call.

Heir? To what? I rubbed my beard, wondering who I could call to have a check done on David. I didn't even know where this man came from, Jerry introduced us. *Jerry.*

I dialed his number next; somebody knew this man's background. He and David at the very least knew each other, and all I needed was a link. "This call better be an apology."

"It ain't. Where Dave come from?"

"Luca, I told you what makes my dick hard—money and pussy. That's it. All this reuniting with long lost relatives ain't got nothing to do with me."

"You introduce me to this man as somebody who I can make a lot of money with, he tells my brother he's actually his father, and now you don't know nothing? That's foul, bruh."

"Listen. I'm a business, man. I'm losing money just having this conversation with you, and since all you trying to get information, this call is over." Jerry was the second person who hung up in my face.

Shit, shit, shit. David wasn't talking, Jerry wasn't talking, and I knew Matteo wasn't trying to hear nothing David had for him. On top of that, Nezz… shit, Nezz. Nezz was on his way to Matteo's to kidnap Sommer. She was my contribution to the family business that I wasn't giving up.

Hmph, fuck Matteo, David, and all that other bullshit. I was about to take what was rightfully mine in the first place.

    Me: You still on track to go pick up that package?

    N.: Almost there now. I'ma text you in a min.

    Me: Aight.

I couldn't wait to see the look on his face when he saw me with his girl. That'll teach his ass to stop taking what was mine just because he was the oldest. I'd even let him have that baby she pregnant with. *After all, I am my brother's keeper.*

Sommer

Soon as Matteo left the house, I was on edge. For some reason I felt like something was going to happen between him and his brother, and I didn't want to be the cause of why they were going through it. Reno did what he could to keep my mind off of what was going on, but he had his own life to worry about.

When I told him I was pregnant, he told me he had a baby on the way too. I guess it was easier explaining to me who he knocked up because I didn't know her, but Matteo and Luca did. According to him, it might cause a rift in their operations, and he didn't exactly know how to handle it. I told him he had to pick a time and place because that was a conversation that needed to be had soon. No man who was a man wanted his son calling another man his father. The way his face lit up when he told me about hearing his son's heartbeat and seeing his face on the ultrasound though… I couldn't wait until our baby was in my arms.

"Reno, I'm going to the house to grab some shoes." I stared out the window in the front room rubbing my little pooch. Matteo wanted to be at my first doctor's appointment, but I told him I'd be ok. In the meantime, Reno offered to come in his absence.

"Shoes? You ain't bring no shoes with you?"

"I didn't grab the ones that go with this dress."

Reno gave me the once over before he headed upstairs. "If you ain't got no shoes to wear with that dress, then change."

"I look cute in this dress though."

"You talking 'bout the dress you ain't got no shoes to wear with, though." Reno shot back quickly. "Put on something else, I ain't going all the way over to Matteo's for some shoes."

"Y'all make me sick," I grumbled, stomping up the steps. "I wanna wear this dress."

"Stop acting so damn spoiled!" he yelled, sounding like his brother.

"I'm telling—" I stopped when Reno's phone interrupted us with a text followed by a phone call.

"Matteo, can I—what? Nah, she here. Who at yo' house? Well, how he get past the gate? How you know? Damn, bro. That's fucked up. Aight, lemme know what you trying to do."

"What happened?" I froze in a panic. Somebody was at my house... I almost went over there for some shoes. Who knew what would've happened?

"Nothing you need to be worried about, we handling it. Come on so the doctor can tell us about this baby."

Matteo wouldn't want me worried, but that didn't stop me from worrying. "Are you gonna tell me what's going on? Who was at my house?" My patience was running thin with these Marino brothers and all these secrets. Every time I turned around, they were having hushed conversations and acting like I wasn't there.

"Ask ya' man, that ain't my place. What is my place is to get you down here to this doctor's appointment and find out about my niece or nephew before my brother get mad."

Texting Matteo three question marks, I grabbed my purse and followed his brother to the car. Bae responded with three kissy-face emojis as if he didn't just call here in a panic. I wasn't gonna do this whole thing over the phone, I knew I'd get better results from him in person anyway.

§

"Sommer, there's no doubt you're almost fourteen weeks," Dr. Lei smiled pleasantly while wiping the gel from my stomach. "Baby's heartbeat is strong, so we know he's healthy. I'm going to prescribe prenatal vitamins for his growth and development, and we need to see you back here in two weeks for the ultrasound, four weeks for your next appointment. Any questions?"

"Just so we're clear, you only heard one heartbeat, right?"

"Yes, boss lady. I know you were concerned with you being a twin that you were pregnant with more than one baby. However, I only heard one heartbeat."

"First and foremost, refer to my son as baby Marino." Matteo spoke up. Reno and I walked in the OB/GYN offices upstairs in my building and he was sitting in the waiting room reading the latest issue of *Parents* magazine. "Second, how do we know he's ok based off his heartbeat? He could have three fingers or frog legs; how can you tell from his heartbeat he's healthy?"

"Mr. Marino, that's why we do the ultrasound," she replied calmly. "In two weeks, we'll see what baby looks like and the sex. Even if your child does have three fingers or frog legs, that doesn't mean he or she won't be healthy."

"But how do you know that though?"

"First-time parent?" We nodded our heads in unison. "I see. Believe it or not, this is common for first-timers. Trust me Mr. Marino, there is nothing to be worried about unless frog legs and three-fingered individuals run in your family."

"I'm not the one passing down Kermit traits baby, so if our child does have that, it came from you." I tittered, pulling my shirt down.

Matteo kissed my forehead, and I noticed a concerned look behind his eyes. "We ain't got no Kermit traits either, babe, so he should be fine."

"She didn't say the baby was a boy, love." I pecked kissed his scruffy chin. "We could very easily be having a girl."

"Clearly she said 'he's healthy', Sommer. I ain't put in all that work for you to be pregnant with a girl out the gate." Matteo raised my shirt and gently rubbed my stomach. "You carrying Matteo Constantine Marino II, that's facts."

"I could very easily be carrying Shannie Celeste Marino too. I put in some work myself that night." I had to remind him even though I was a virgin, I still listened when

Torrie talked about what freaky tricks she had that drove her husband crazy.

"How pregnant did you say we was, Doc?"

"Almost fourteen weeks, give or take—"

"What's that on a real calendar?"

"Three and a half… almost four months," she chuckled.

"Oh, yeah, that was that first night then." Matteo nodded smugly. "You might've contributed, but I definitely gave you this di—"

"MATTEO!"

"Had you screaming just like that too, only a little louder." He put a hand out to help me off the examining table.

"Dr. Lei don't wanna hear all that!" I punched his arm, he played too much.

"Believe me Sommer, I've heard worse," she smiled while passing me a prescription. "I'll give you the same spiel I give all my new mommies: you can have that filled at your local pharmacy, or if there's another brand you prefer, that's fine. Whatever you decide, make sure you're taking your vitamins once a day, every day in the morning with orange juice so your system absorbs it better. Wait, I don't have to tell you this, I work for you," Elizabeth chuckled again. "I'll see you guys in a month, ok?"

"Ok," we replied in unison. "Stop copying me, Matteo," I punched him again.

"I don't know why I didn't realize before you two are married. It's obvious now," Dr Lei remarked, walking out of the exam room.

"Don't be embarrassing me in front of your employees, Sommer." Matteo grabbed my butt first and moved up to my waist so he could pull me closer to him. "Got the doctor thinking I didn't lock and load this thang right here."

"Whatever, Mr. Marino. Anyway, who was at my house earlier?" We walked out of the doctor's office together holding hands.

"Nobody."

I stopped short on the sidewalk, hand on my hip. "So now we lying?"

"Can I finish?" Matteo reached out and pulled me closer to him. "Nobody you need to be worried about."

"I shouldn't be worried, huh? Well, I'm about to go home then." I waited on the sidewalk for him to open my door once we got to the truck.

"No, the fuck you ain't." Matteo's tone was remarkably calm. "House ain't safe right now."

"See, I knew something was going on! Why you keep shutting me out?"

"Do you know what would happen if something happened to you, Sommer? You my world, ain't nobody safe out here if I lose you. I can't take that chance."

"And you're the air I breathe. What makes you think I want to take that kind of chance with you, Matteo?" I spoke my truth. "You're my only family until this baby comes out. I want you there, not FaceTiming from prison or Reno talking about how proud you *would've* been."

"Sommer, nothing—"

"That's what you say, Matteo, but look at the life you live—"

"I was in the life when you met me, Sommer."

"And I only met that Matteo briefly. The man I know is a gentleman who loves on me and only me! You said it's us against the world, right?"

"We are, what you mean?"

"Yet I can't go home, you and Reno been whispering in corners ever since you been at his house, and now you and Luca fell out. When does it end?"

Matteo sighed once we got to the stoplight, and I could tell by his facial expression he was choosing his words. "Luca went into a partnership with Sleazo against my advice, and now the nigga he working with claim he my real pops."

"Wha-what? How is that possible? And who is Sleazo?"

"My father died when we was kids; Reno shot him in the head by accident on his seventh birthday. Right now, who Sleazo is doesn't matter."

"Oh my God!"

"Yeah, so now this David person wanna meet up with me to talk," he finished once the light turned green. We rode down the street in silence; I was in shock at what I just heard. Reno told me stories about how close they used to be, but now looking at them, you couldn't tell Luca and Matteo were related. Nor that Reno was carrying around the burden of killing his father.

"Are you going to talk to him?"

"No."

"Why not?"

"What I'm supposed to say? I ain't never heard of this nigga until the other day, now... man, naw. Much shit as we went through in that house after Pop died... it's too late. It's too late, man." Matteo spoke with finality.

"Baby, you should at least hear him out. Maybe he is, maybe he isn't. At the very least, get a DNA test to see if you're related, and go from there. If he is, you need to know his family history so I'm not out here giving birth to Kermit the frog for real."

Matteo glanced at me sideways before he busted out laughing. "Aye, don't be talking 'bout my baby like that. 'Whether he has frog legs or not, he'll still be a healthy baby'," he called himself mimicking my OB/GYN.

"Shiiii… y'all can have that healthy baby, I'm out." I threw up the peace sign, scrunching my lips so he knew I wasn't playing with him or Dr. Lei. Matteo fine and all, but if he got all these tadpoles out here waiting to see the light of day, I wasn't gonna be a part of it.

"Listen, baby, I'll call the man, aight?" Matteo scrolled through his phone and hit talk. Since his Bluetooth was connected to the truck, the call popped up on the console; I'd been forced to listen to the car read his text messages more than once. As the phone rang in the car's speakers, I glanced at the console and saw an overseas number on the screen.

"Allo? Matteo?"

"Aye, meet me on the lakefront so we can have this conversation."

"Where and what time?"

"You know where Veteran's Park is?"

"I'll find it. What time?"

"'Bout an hour. That'll give me time to drop wife off—"

"Drop me off? Oh no, hunny, I'm coming too!"

"Hold on a sec." Matteo put the call on mute before turning his attention to me. "No big mama, you gotta go home."

"You said I can't go to my house, and I'm not going to Reno's without you."

"Sommer—"

"Matteo." I rolled my eyes first before focusing on his face.

"I don't like you no mo'," he huffed, taking the phone off mute.

"I don't like you either, but you heard what I said."

"Aye, wife coming too," he shot another sideways glance in my direction before shaking his head.

"Thank you, Matteo. I'd love to meet your wife."

"We bringing a DNA kit too. That's not a problem, is it?" I yelled out, snickering at Matteo's sour face.

"No, please do. I didn't expect you to take my word for it. You're what, thirty-two now, right, Matteo?"

"Look, we'll see you in an hour." Matteo hit end on their call as we pulled into the CVS parking lot. "I can't do this, man."

"Why?"

"This nigga… I can't do this, man! Pop been dead for twenty-two years! I been taking care of my brothers for twenty-two years! Now this nigga come along and say those ain't my full-blooded brothers, they my half-brothers?" he expressed, pounding on the steering wheel.

"Matteo, whole or half, Luca and Reno are still your brothers! But you owe it to not only you, but to your baby to know your heritage."

"You right," my future husband sighed, dragging weathered hands down his face. "You right. This just some crazy shit, nobody refers to my mother as Tamiko. The fact that he knew her name, man… just the fact he knew her name…"

"Your mom's name is Tamiko?"

"Yeah, why?"

"Oh, no reason," I fidgeted with my phone, my father's message flashing in my mind's eye. "I'm sure it's just a coincidence."

"What's a coincidence?" Matteo pressed.

"No, my dad said my mom's best friend's name was Tamiko too. That's funny, right? Two black women named Tamiko who lived in Milwaukee at the same time." I giggled nervously to myself. *She couldn't be…*

"What did you say your mother's name was?"

"Kayla."

"Auntie Kayla?"

"Auntie? Matteo, don't tell me—"

"No, she wasn't my real auntie." Matteo put his hands up, laughing. "She was my mother's best friend, used to come around from time to time. Last time I saw her was at—aw, hell naw."

"What, Matteo? When was the last time you saw her?"

"Reno's seventh birthday party."

Matteo

For Milwaukee to be as big as it was, this really was a small town. Maybe it was time for me to leave, finding out our parents knew one another was fucking with my head. I never knew Auntie Kayla had kids, especially not two twin daughters. Never could anybody have told me back then twenty-two years later, I'd be burying one of those daughters while the other one was pregnant with my first kid.

"Uhmm… let's just go see what this David person has to say for himself, and then go from there." Sommer spoke quietly after I got back from grabbing the DNA kit.

"Yeah."

We pulled up to the park on the lakefront five minutes ahead of time, and David was already there. Putting my irritation to the side because Sommer asked me to, I got out and opened her door first before we walked hand in hand to meet the man who claimed he was my biological father.

"Nice to meet you under more pleasant circumstances." David began. "Last time we met was a little hectic, eh?"

"Let's go over here and sit down. Wife pregnant." I spoke quietly, ushering Sommer to a bench near the water to sit. "Talk to me, Dave."

"Hmm, where should I start?"

"The beginning would be nice." Sommer spoke snidely, which was out of character, especially for her.

"Of course. Jerry introduced me to your mother at a day party—"

"A day party." I shared my disparaging opinion about Milwaukee's shadiest businessman, shaking my head. "Jerry and the muthafuckin' day parties. Ol' bastard don't do nothing at night?"

"Well, according to Jerry, nighttime was reserved for—"

"Forget I asked. Continue, man."

"Tamiko was a very attractive woman. The minute she and her friend Kayla walked in, every man—" he stopped for a second and took a deep breath. "Every man in there wanted her. Kayla walked in behind her looking—."

"David, I don't know you, but I'm also not gonna sit here and allow you to speak negatively about my mother," Sommer turned to David with a raised eyebrow. If looks could kill, his heart would've stopped.

"I never said she—Matteo, who is this?"

"It's complicated, man. I just found out myself about twenty minutes ago," I explained.

"Matteo's wife. He told you exactly who I was before we pulled up," Sommer uncrossed her legs and I scooted closer to her. My little doctor had a mean streak sometimes, and I didn't need them arguing, because I already knew who's side I was taking. "Kayla is my mother, and if I find out—" I saw the squint in her eyes as she pointed at Dave, scooting closer before I stopped her. Sommer was about to kill that man with her bare hands.

"No, I—I wasn't going to say anything negative," he backtracked. "You're a lot like her as a matter of fact." David smiled, hoping to calm her down. "I was about to say equally as beautiful. She just wasn't interested in any of the men at the party, that's all."

"Yeah, you betta had." Sommer nodded, scooting backwards on the bench. "Hate to see your James Bond looking ass floating in this lake. Somebody should've told you Matteo don't play about me."

"Sommer?"

"What?"

"Girl, sit down and let this man finish his story." I reached out and rubbed her leg to help soothe her nerves.

"Can I continue?" David questioned, snickering at both of us.

"Yeah, go ahead, man."

"Matteo, as you know, Jerry's day parties are nothing more than connecting women with men for a specific 'service'," he air quoted slyly. I knew what he meant: Sleazo was a pimp who didn't check for ID. "Me and Tamiko exchanged phone numbers, and we... 'connected' a few times. We weren't exclusive, but I was a little offended when she told me she couldn't see me anymore because she was getting married."

"How long had y'all been 'connecting' before she told you that?"

"Me and Tamiko saw each other whenever I was in the States, so on and off… about three years," David admitted.

"And in three years, you didn't know she was in a whole relationship?"

"Like I said, we only saw each other when I was here. We didn't do the phone for hours at a time, we weren't sending letters every week, no 'I love yous' exchanged. No feelings involved. We was just…"

"Just what?"

"Connect buddies."

"Connect buddies?" Sommer interrupted again. "What is a connect buddy?"

"I think he saying they were fuck buddies, baby." I saved David from getting punched in the jaw, yet appreciated he didn't call the situation what it was.

"Ooouuu, ok."

"We hooked up one more time before she got married, then she moved and changed her number. I was back at Jerry's day parties and bumped into Kayla sometime later who told me she thought Tamiko's oldest son Matteo favored me. I waved it off, but she was serious."

"Baby, now that he mentions it, you do kinda—"

"I ain't trying to hear that shit. Let's do this test so we can go our separate ways." I waved both of them off, heading back to the truck to get the DNA test. My phone was flashing with Luca's number on the screen, but I wasn't in the right frame of mind mentally to hear what he was talking about. Walking back to where they sat chatting away, I had no doubt they exchanged phone numbers to talk later. David knew about both of our mothers' secret lives. I didn't care, but Sommer seemed genuinely curious.

"I'll open it for you." Sommer volunteered, seeing how I sat staring at the bag with my mind somewhere else. I'd been Matteo Constantine Marino my whole life, but now there was a possibility I wasn't. I had another man's name attached to mine who I probably wasn't no kin to. Who the fuck was I then?

We did the test and sealed everything up, making sure all boxes were checked and signatures in place. "Ok, now what?"

"I'll take this down to FedEx. The sooner they get it, the sooner they can process it and let us know." Sommer spoke up. "That way, we know who's who and what's what."

I stared at the man who claimed to be my father, sucking my teeth as he smiled brightly. "Until then, I don't think we have anything else to talk about, bruh. If you ain't, then it ain't no love lost."

"And if I am?" David questioned squarely.

"We already thirty-two years in without speaking, so let's go for thirty-two more." I turned my back to him, hoping he got the hint.

"MATTEO! Don't say that!" Sommer yelled from behind me.

"Fuck that nigga, man! You knew about me when I was a kid, but thirty-two years later, you decide we should have a relationship? Man… Renato Achilles Marino Sr. will ALWAYS be my father! That's been the man who was always there, and if it wasn't for little bro, he'd STILL be here! Fuck him!" I roared, walking swiftly back to my truck. Sommer knew I was pissed.

Climbing in on the driver's side, I slammed my door, watching Sommer and David continue their conversation as he escorted her to my vehicle. *That's the least you can do*, I thought, watching them exchange a small hug before he opened her door. She waved at him one last time before I started up the truck and tried to run his ass over.

"MATTEO! Don't hit David!" Sommer screamed just as I swerved in the opposite direction.

"Why you so friendly and concerned about his well-being?" I growled. "He trying to 'connect' with you too?"

"Yeah, but not the way you making it seem. Matteo, I know you're upset—"

"Oh, you a mind reader now?"

Sommer stared at me for a minute before she turned around and grabbed her purse from the back seat. "You know what? You can let me out at this next corner coming up."

"Where the fuck you going?"

"I'm not in the mood for you and your fucked-up attitude, Matteo! He knew my mother too!"

"Oh, yeah? Did he fuck your mother too? Was Auntie Kayla one of his fuck buddies? You got a little brother or sister out here that you ain't know nothing about!"

"I don't know what they did, I wasn't there! He probably did fuck my mother, I don't know! I know it ain't nothing me or you can do about something that happened over thirty years ago, Matteo! That ain't got nothing to do with us!"

"Lemme ask you this, Sommer." I pulled over at the next corner and threw the car in park. "You so dead set on me and him getting to know each other, be friends and shit. He know your mother too. Who your pops?"

"What?"

"You heard me. You taking up for this man and for all you know we could be brother and sister."

Sommer stared at me for a second with a look on her face like she was about to punch me in the mouth before she got out of my truck and slammed the door. "FUCK YOU MATTEO!"

"FUCK YOU, SOMMER!" I snapped back while pulling away from the curb. All this caring and sensitive shit was being directed at the wrong person, if I didn't fuck with somebody she wasn't supposed to either.

I got to the next corner and heard someone screaming my name. Of course I looked around first before checking the rearview. A black Riviera was at the curb where Sommer was standing a minute before. I threw the truck in reverse, hit the gas, and lurched backward. Sommer was swinging her arms for a second before some nigga reached up and punched her in the face. I crashed into a car I didn't realize was behind me as a second nigga tossed her in the backseat of the car.

Reaching for the door handle, I couldn't get out fast enough. As soon as my feet hit the pavement, I took off running, ignoring the ringing in my ears. Both men hopped in the front seat of the Riviera and bussed a U-turn in the middle of the street before speeding off in the opposite direction.

Everything...nothing meant shit to me. These muthafuckas really kidnapped my girl and my kid.

"SOMMER! WHAT THE FUCK, MAN!"

Luca

"You got her?"

"Yeah. She in the back seat, boss man," Nezz replied curtly.

"Bring her out here to the other spot."

"Bet. You got my money?"

"Of course I got yo' money. Have I ever flaked on you before?"

"Just saying. You ain't got my money, I ain't dropping her back off." he jeered. "This wifey in the back seat."

"Just bring her. I got yo' money, my nigga."

"Aight." Nezz hung up just in time, because I'd just walked in the stash house to get Sommer's ransom money. It was only right her so-called 'husband' paid for it. Reno too, but the past few months Matteo been the money man, so his contribution was the biggest. Tapping the buttons on the digital safe in the study, I smiled when the green light flashed. Opening the door to all that—air? "The fuck? We got robbed?"

I practiced that patience thing after I hit talk on Reno's number waiting the two seconds for him to pick up. "Luca, now isn't the best time to—"

"Oh, you and Matteo 'bout to go get our money back? Where y'all at?"

"Wait, what money? What you talking bout, Luca?"

"Ain't we supposed to be meeting up at the stash house today? I'm already out here." I almost forgot who I was talking to, Reno would pull up immediately if he thought we was broke.

"Yeah, but you saying we got robbed? What block?"

"Uhhh—aye, lemme call you back and get the exact details from this lil' nigga." I hung up, hoping he didn't make a few calls to find out what I was talking about. This double life shit was crazy.

I unplugged the cameras from the house a while back so Matteo and Reno wouldn't see me taking money from the stash. I'd ran out of money in my own account from maintaining my current lifestyle after Matteo's pops flaked on me that one day. Mad at him, Matteo, and Sommer, I went and blew 25k in the casino that night and been trying to make my money back ever since. I needed that money, and even with me doing the internet thing myself, I still wasn't making enough to contribute. Jerry fucked me up when he took Keedra's video off that website, my first check was for 10k. So I'd come out here and get a few thousand out the safe every now and then. Matteo wouldn't say nothing about me getting a couple of dollars, but if he found out I'd been grabbing 10k a day for the past month, sometimes 20 depending on how my day was going, he might be upset.

On top of that, I was paying Nezz out of the stash too. I couldn't go pull 50k out of my account because it wasn't there, and the man still had to be compensated for his services. Reno and Matteo just needed to understand that our bond as each other's keeper was them maintaining my lifestyle as Luca Marino until I got back on. I couldn't be out here looking broke; I had a reputation.

The bigger issue was Sommer. No matter where he was in the city, it was gonna take about twenty minutes to get to the spot, and I needed to come up with 100k in that time span. "Lemme call Reno back," I mumbled, not knowing what he had going on and not really giving a fuck. "Aye, lil' bro."

"Did you find out who robbed us?"

"Nah, false alarm. Aye, you got any money on you?"

"Not on me, but I can get to some. How much you need?"

"'Bout 100k."

"A hunnit? What you need a hundred thousand dollars for, Luca?"

"Why you questioning me? I can't get 100k just cause?"

"With everything that's happened in the past hour, naw muthafucka, you can't get shit just cause," Matteo growled in my ear. "Where the fuck is my wife, Luca?"

"You married? Aye, congrats, bro. My bad for not getting you and the wife a wedding gift."

Matteo chuckled darkly in my ear, and I knew it was up whenever he pulled up. "One, two... Matteo's coming for you... three, four... gonna kick down your door. Five, six... betta get your shit... seven, eight… be glad you ain't moving weight… nine, ten… never fucking with you again, bitch!" he sang eerily before hanging up.

N: Where you at, my nig?

Me*: OMW now*

Much money as I already gave him, shit Nezz should be paying me. I left the house and hopped in the Jag, speeding to the meet up spot, I wasn't worried about it, what could he do?

§

"'Bout time you got here, nigga!" Me and Nezz shook up in the middle of the street. "I been trying to wake shawty up since we grabbed her, but she must've been tired-tired."

I stepped over to the black Riviera with the tinted windows and peeked in the back seat, taking note of the fresh bruise on her eye. "What's that on her face?"

"Man, yo' brother must be using her as his punching bag or something, I'on know," the nigga with Nezz was quick to speak up first. "You got that lil' money though?"

"Do I got the money? Y'all out here beating on my girl and you asking me 'bout some money?"

"You said snatch her up, that's what we did. Cost extra if you don't want her touched." Nezz stuck a piece of gum in his mouth and looked around absently. "Like my people said, you got that lil' money?"

"I ain't have a chance to get to the bank—"

"Aye, this nigga ain't got no money!" Nezz's associate tapped him twice on the arm, and they both walked back to the Riviera. Sliding in the driver's side, I saw the window roll down as he started up the car. "Luca!"

"Wait—lemme go to the—"

"You can come pick yo' girl up from Decatur, GA when you get me my money. Oh, for every day we have her, it's an extra thou on top of that hunnit." Nezz pulled off without another word, his dual pipes guzzling down the street.

I had Sommer kidnapped to spite my brother. The plan was to hold her for a couple of days while I convinced Matteo to see things my way so we could get back to getting this money. Him and Reno was supposed to make the drop last night so I'd have the money to pay the ransom and they didn't. On top of that, I don't know how, but he knew I had something to do with it. My brother was gonna kill me over a bitch. *I'll be ready for him when he pull up.*

Reno

Matteo's truck was sitting directly in front of my front steps, he missed the driveway and the garage completely. I thought Sommer was being extra and not wanting to walk on the concrete, but when he got out the truck slamming the door so hard it cracked his windshield, I started grabbing the guns. "Aye, you think he was following you?"

"It don't e'en matter. All that matters is me shooting these niggas head off. That's it." Matteo shoved two pistols on either side of his waist, tucking one in the holster on his ankle before grabbing the keys to the truck. "Nigga been scheming and stealing this whole time, but I'm the angry one when I go choke this nigga out. Yeah, aight."

"I'm going too, bro. Luca crossed the line this time, some shit you just don't do."

We rode out to Luca's townhouse he didn't know we knew about down in Racine. I rode with him, because truth be told, we were both ready to kill Luca. Wasn't no talking some sense into him, Sommer was a sweetheart. She gave me a female's perspective and didn't tell me what I wanted to hear. Sommer gave it to me blood raw, and I needed that. Once we wrapped up this Luca thing, it was time for me to tell Matteo about my son and my baby mama.

"Right here." I pointed at the complex on the right side. "That sign say Lighthouse Point, right?"

"Yeah."

"Yeah, he in the back. Should see that black truck of his or that raggedy ass Jag." Matteo looked from left to right as we drove. "There he go."

"You know he parked in front of his house, right?" I checked the pistol to make sure it was still on safety.

"That's ya brother, Mr. *'Don't Nobody Know Where I Stay So I'ma Park In Front Of The Spot'* face ass." Matteo parked four houses down and threw the car in park. "Let's go see if this nigga want some company."

We crept around the back and hopped the fence. Sliding the metal piece in between the patio doors, we jiggled the lock and heard a click. Once the door popped open, we eased the glass aside and crept quietly inside. Even in the upper-class projects, Luca still had Picassos on the wall and cashmere rugs on the floors, so we had a buffer to move about the townhouse as we pleased. I found Luca in a bedroom upstairs by himself passed out on the bed naked with a half empty bag of coke lying next to him. Everything made sense; no wonder he was acting like he'd lost his mind lately.

Texting Matteo, I took the pistol off safety in case he decided to wake up and start shooting. "Oh for real? THIS what we doing, Luca!" My oldest brother stepped in the room and looked around with his nose turned up.

"Wha—Matteo!" Luca cheered. He called himself trying to jump up and fell flat on his face. "Where Maria at? Somebody need to clean this damn house!" He held the wall to balance himself while trying a second time to get on his feet.

"Is that coke on ya nose, bro?" I used my pistol to point out the obvious. "Who you copping from?"

"These Kenosha niggas got some great powder, man. We need—" he sniffed and pinched his nose, "We need to link up with them!"

"Luca, I'ma ask you this one time and one time only. You don't answer, and I can't control what happens next..." Matteo rested his pistol on our brother's temple and cocked it. "Where Sommer at, bro?"

"Sommer?" Luca giggled. "SOMMER MY NIGGA? You came all the way out here looking for Sommer?" he roared sardonically. "Yo' bitch—ooops... can't call her that can I? She wifey, right?" he sniffed, pinching his nose and blinking rapidly. His bloodshot red eyes stared at Matteo with disgust while he wiped his nose with the back of his hand. "'Wifey'," he whined, "is on her way to Decatur," he jabbed a second time.

"Decatur? As in Illinois?"

"As in Georgia, my nigga!" Luca roared. "Matteo, put that gun down fo' you hurt yaself. You ain't gonna do shit! You yo' brother's keeper, right? RIGHT!"

"This nigga gone." I lowered my piece. Seeing the look in my older brother's eye, however, I knew I had to say something. "Didn't you say you can't kill an innocent crackhead?"

"This crackhead ain't innocent." Matteo pulled the trigger before I could stop him, and Luca's brains splattered like the sun's rays peeking over the horizon on the wall behind him. "Pass me his phone."

I stepped over Luca's body on the floor in a crumpled heap, reaching for his phone on the bed. Snatching the phone, Matteo unlocked it and scrolled through his text messages before he found what he was looking for. "Aye, we gotta pray over this nigga before we go."

"You right." Matteo cleared his throat and bowed his head. "Dear Lord, forgive us of our trespasses. Bless us, oh Lord, for we have sinned. And if you see in our hearts that we're out for revenge, please blame it on the son of the morning. Amen."

"Amen. Let's go, it's a long ride down to Decatur."

"Facts." My brother took the silencer off his pistol, reloading while I made sure I had my wallet in case we needed a hotel room. "Think we should call a cleanup crew?"

"Yeah. After all, he is family."

"Aight." Matteo sent a text from Luca's phone to his people, then broke it in half with his bare hands. "Somebody coming to get his ass."

§

Watching the lights from the city roll by as we drove through Chicago's south side, I figured it was time for me to tell Matteo about me and Tamra. Xander was a four-star elite general on the streets, not to mention the only other person Matteo trusted outside of us. "Aye."

"Yea."

"Doc let y'all hear the heartbeat?"

"Yeah," he smiled. My brother was already a proud father and the baby wasn't even here yet. "That was some crazy shit. I never thought I'd be nobody's father for real, man." Matteo cheesed as we drove under the 95th Street overpass. "Look, Reno, Luca—"

"As messed up as it is, bro, I understand. Luca tried to make you choose between him and your legacy, and that's some weak shit, for real. Somewhere in his mind, I think he believed you don't deserve to be happy unless we good first."

"I think you right, man." Matteo merged onto the toll road toward Indiana. "Every time we talked, it was, 'am I my brother's keeper?' Like it was something I wasn't doing, like somewhere I was slacking."

"You know he was saying that shit to me too? I mean, yeah I fell into the trap for a minute, he got to me. Had me coming at you with that whole 'remember our oath' thing. Aye, bruh, that ain't us. For real, you got your own life to live, it ain't our business what you do with it."

"Sommer said something like that about her sister before they—" he shook his head before he continued, "Well, you see what happened with them."

"And I see what happened with you and Sommer. How you stepped up and became your woman's keeper. I'm proud of you, man."

"Thanks, bruh." We rode down the expressway, both lost in our own thoughts.

"Matteo. Bruh, you ain't the only one of us with a baby on the way, man."

"Aw, straight up? Congrats, bro!" He shook my shoulder with one hand. "Who's the lucky woman?"

"Uhmm…"

"Uhmm? I don't know uhmm, bro."

"Tamra."

"Tamra?" Matteo pulled to the side of the road and put the car in park. "Tamra who?"

"Man—" I rubbed a hand across my waves before rubbing down my face.

"I'm—Reno, yo' ass too muthafuckin' sneaky for me," he laughed heartily, shaking his head. "Xander know you been tearing that pussy up?"

"Shiiit, I don't know how he don't know!" I cackled along with my brother, dapping him up. "You know they fall in love with that Marino dick, that left hook get 'em every time!"

"BIG facts!" Matteo put the car in drive and pulled back on the road. "You telling me I need to kill my top dog? Because if he come for you, I'm coming for him."

"What Luca used to say? 'I got a little brother too'? That's me, bro. I am Luca's little brother. I ain't worried about X."

"Aight. Tamra what, five… six months?"

"Yeah."

"Bet. I can't wait, man!" He started beating on the steering wheel again, cackling loudly. "Aye, why we ain't fly out here? This a long ass ride!"

"That adrenaline, man." I shook my head in agreement. "Plus, who gonna pick us up from the airport?"

"Shit, don't you got Waze on ya phone? Aye, book us on the next flight out of Indy!"

"Man…" I logged onto Delta's website, and it wasn't nothing leaving until the morning. "By the time the plane land, we'll be there!"

"Yeah, I ain't 'bout to be sleeping in no airport either, so fuck it."

"Aye, wake me up when we get to Kentucky. I'll drive some then."

"Aight."

Sommer

One minute, I was cussing Matteo out and the next minute, I woke up to the smell of weed and loud music. Two men I never seen before were in the front seat cussing and smoking while the car swerved across...wait, where were we going?

"I GOTTA PEE!" I tried screaming over the loud music, hoping one of them heard me. My face hurt, and I didn't know why.

"What you say, baby? You gotta pee?" the driver questioned, passing the blunt to the passenger before he turned the music down.

"Uhmm... yes. Please."

We came off at the next exit and pulled into a gas station so I could relieve my bladder. I checked the mirror and saw my face was actually swollen; one of these bastards hit me. My stomach started growling when I walked out the bathroom, and I remembered Matteo was supposed to get me something to eat when we left the doctor's office before we got caught up with David.

I grabbed a hot dog off the roller and added some chili and cheese. Since they seemed to think this whole kidnapping thing was cute, one of these men was paying for my food. Matteo gave me some money earlier, but that was the least they could do.

"You hungry?" the driver questioned, looking at my hot dog, three bags of chips, two juices, and water.

"Starving. Grab me two Hershey bars with almonds too."

"Eating like you pregnant or something." The driver called himself trying to be funny, pulling out a wad of money. "Gimme this and $45 on pump twelve." He paid for my stuff and got his change before turning back to me. "How you that little eating like that?"

"Cause I am pregnant. And even if I wasn't, I got a high metabolism." I took a bite out of my hot dog and walked back to the car.

"You pregnant, lil' mama? For real, for real?"

"Yeah, for real, for real." I opened my own door and was about to climb in the back seat until the driver stopped me.

"Sit up here, I can't have you in the back seat. Aye bruh, apologize to my baby mama for punching her in the face!"

His baby mama? Oh, hell naw—
"Uhmm, I need to call my doctor. My stomach been cramping for about an hour." I lied, hoping he'd give me my phone so I could text Matteo. I had an app on my phone that I was sure he was tracking by now, but

if he wasn't, I needed to let him know to pull it up.

"You can't take some Tylenol? My first baby mama almost overdosed on some damn ibuprofen. You can't take that?"

"My pregnancy high risk." I lied again, hoping karma didn't come back to bite me in the ass. "My doctor told me don't take nothing without running it by her first."

"Why you eating all that junk then?" the second man spat, trying to make me feel guilty for eating chips and candy.

"Look around you! This ain't Whole Foods! I'm hungry, what you think I'm supposed to eat?" I snapped before biting my chili dog.

"Here," the driver reached in the armrest and passed me my phone. "Make sure you calling the doctor, don't try no bullshit."

"When it comes to the health of my baby, I ain't got time to be playing games with you and nobody else." I opened the messages app on my phone and hit record. "Hey Dr. Wu, this is Sommer. I'm calling because I'm having some cramping, and I'm on my way out of town. If you can, call me back with a doctor I can go see in—" I pretended like I was hitting the hold button and turned to the driver. "Where we at?"

"Right now we in Tennessee, but we on our way to Atlanta." this dummy spoke up first.

"I'm in Tennessee on the interstate, but I'm on my way to Atlanta. Haven't seen a hospital, but if you can find me near I-75 south should be fine. Thanks, Dr. Wu." I hit send and locked my phone, passing it back to him. Hopefully Matteo would make the connection that I was on the highway and turn on the app so he could track exactly where I was.

"You think your boyfriend Luca gonna get that money up for you?" the second man questioned from the back seat. "We ain't gonna keep you that long, if he don't call in three days, you an' that baby gonna be floating in the Chattahoochee."

"What's the Chattahoochee?"

"River. I advise you call your baby daddy," the second man mocked dryly.

"Luca isn't my child's father. Who told y'all that?"

"He did," the driver raised his eyebrow, confused. "Wait, do you know who Luca is?"

"Yeah, I know him. He's my brother-in-law."

"Brother-in-law? Matteo's *wife*?"

"Oh, so you know my husband?"

"Do I—aye, we ain't going back to Milwaukee," the driver shook his head as he drove.

"Told you, man! I told you! Ain't shit up there but a bunch of weak niggas and—"

"Uhmm… my husband ain't a 'weak nigga'." I air quoted.

"You just saying that cause you carrying that nigga's seed." The driver waved me off. "All them Marino niggas ain't on shit."

We'll see who on what when my husband show up, dummy. "If you say so… I'm sorry, I didn't catch your name."

"Nezz."

"And you?"

"Streets know me as Amp, as in Amp some shit up!" he yelled, taking two puffs from the blunt in his hand.

"Nezz and Amp." I pointed at each man to make sure I had their names right for when my husband showed up. They were both idiots, not only was I sitting in the front seat with the window down letting my hair blow, but Nezz let me use my phone, being all caring and sensitive because I was pregnant. *What if I was lying, dumb ass?* "Why we going to Atlanta?"

"We from Atlanta." Amp spoke up with his chatty self. "Actually Decatur."

"So y'all kidnap pregnant women all the time down here, huh?"

"For $100k we do."

"Luca didn't give y'all $100k for me?"

"Nah, said he needed more time." Nezz watched the road as he spoke.

"Well, did you call my husband? I know he'll give it to you."

"I'm sure he would—wait…did you call Matteo?"

"Nah, we just found out that's her husband. I was trying to get that extra 3k."

"But if that's the case and you thought me and Luca were together, why not just call Matteo to see if he wanted to get his sister-in-law back?"

They looked at each other stupidly; I was over Dumb and Dumber already.

"Uhmm…we got other business with Matteo and didn't wanna confuse the two," Amp stuttered.

"Oh, ok." I turned my gaze back to the window so they didn't see the look on my face. *Oh my God, I wonder if they share a brain too.* "How long before we get there?"

"About four hours." Nezz lit up another blunt and took a long pull.

"Hmph. Never been to Georgia." *I hope I'm there to see what Matteo do to y'all when he see my face though.*

"Oh, you gonna like it." Amp took the blunt from Nezz and started babysitting. "Strip clubs, good food, parties—"

"I don't do none of that, I mostly just hang out with my husband." I huffed, watching the world speed by at 80mph. "Y'all can have all that."

"Aw, we got a real one!" Nezz got hyped, bouncing back and forth in his seat. "Yeah, Ma Dukes gonna love you!"

I wonder if bae gonna kill her too... "Is she cooking?"

"I'll make sure she have you something to eat, pretty face." Nezz touched my cheek, and it took every fiber of my being not to smack his hand off my skin.

"Thanks, Nezz." I smiled innocently, knowing what they had coming on the horizon. *They 'bout to get on my nerves.* I rubbed my little heartbeat and... wait... was that a hand? *Oh, baby! Mommy felt that! Matteo, my love, where are you?*

Keedra

I hadn't heard anything from Nezz, Luca, or Matteo in the past twenty-four hours, and I was getting desperate. As a matter of fact, nobody seen or heard anything from anybody, which was a surprise. Jerry didn't even have any information from me when I went over his house for our weekly date. Yeah, I went over there and told him we couldn't see each other a couple of weeks ago. Rekindling my relationship with Matteo was taking longer than I thought, and I was running low on money, so I gave Jerry a call.

"Keedra, you need to get a job." My mother burst in my room every morning and irritated the shit out of me. "You can't keep laying up round here sleeping all day and out all night."

"I got an interview today." I lied. I wasn't getting no damn job; she talked that same shit every week. I had $3,000 in my purse from last night in the club, and the day was still young. Plus, I had VIP at the strip club, which was a guaranteed $5,000. As long as I was living at her house for free, I didn't need no job.

"You betta hope they hire you because yo' free ride is slowly coming to the end of the road, hunny!"

"Whatever, Ma. Lemme go get ready for this—Damn, Ma! You just gonna kick me in my fuckin' back?"

"Who you whatevering, lil' bitch!" my mother spat. "Don't start that shit, Keedra!"

"How I'm supposed to go to the interview with you bruising my damn back!"

"You betta wrap some Saran Wrap around you and go to that damn interview!" she shrieked shrilly. "I mean it, Keedra!"

"I'm going, damn!" I got up off the steps, snatched my keys off the mantel, and walked out of her house. I was over my free ride already, but when I left her house, I'd be going back to my mansion in Brookfield, thanks to our little fake baby.

As soon as I got in the car, I hit talk on Sheena's number. "Whaddup, bitch. Ma Dukes must be pissing you off again, huh?"

This hoe knew me too well. "Girl, I can't wait until I get back home. What you doing?"

"Waiting on these niggas to go home so I can clean this house. Girl, be glad you stay witcho mama and she don't let you have company." Sheena low key called herself coming for me, but I'd still drag her all over Milwaukee. "Every night they be over here smoking and shit."

"Hmph, what y'all 'bout to do today?" I turned on the ignition and pulled into traffic.

"Shit. Saw a flyer for this day party yo' sugar daddy throwing on IG, so I might go to that."

"My sugar daddy?"

"Jerry," Sheena cackled hoeishly in my ear. "Shit, I'm broke too."

"If that's the case, you should go." I put on my turn signal, then changed my mind. "You can make a lot of money at his parties." I knew what happened at Jerry's day parties, hence the reason I stopped going. Plus, we were exclusive... at least we were when I wasn't tied up with David, Ronnie, or Matteo. "What happened with that one thing I asked you to do?"

"Oh, send Matteo's wife that sonogram? I did it."

"Bitch, I know you did it," I sucked my teeth at this scandalous ass bitch. Sheena would do anything if the thought she was getting some money or to start some shit.

"I'm trying to see if she said something back."

"Nope."

"Nothing?"

"Nothing."

"Lil' bum bitch. She act like she the only one Matteo can get pregnant, like she the only one he fucking—"

"Wait, Matteo still—"

"Girl, yeah." I lied. "Regardless of what he do on the street, my baby know where home is."

"Do he?"

"Excuse me?"

"I said he shole do! Lemme let you go; I gotta make sure these niggas ain't stealing food out my house. Call me later, love!" Sheena hurried off the phone.

I needed to get my shit together for real. In order for me to do so, I had to be out of Milwaukee and back in the suburbs where I truly belonged. Instead of my original destination, I hit the expressway and headed toward Brookfield. I didn't care how long it took, I was gonna be there when he got home so we could talk. Maybe he did call me someone else's name the last time we had sex, but today was the day I was telling his 'wife' the truth about her husband.

§

Luca's phone went to voice mail for the fifth time that day, and I was beginning to get worried. We'd never gone this long without some form of communication, even if it was just a text message. I would've called Reno, but I wasn't in the mood to be interrogated about how I got his number and why I was calling. I just needed to wait.

My phone vibrated in the cup holder, and I grabbed it before it hit the floor. "Hey Nezz."

"Aye, you told this nigga Matteo where I live?"

"Did I—no! I don't even know where you live!"

"Where that nigga Luca?" he questioned, sucking his teeth.

"I haven't talked to Luca. Wait, you saying—hello? Nezz?" I checked my phone and saw he hung up.

> *Me: Where Nezz from?*
>
> *Jerry: Why you wanna know?*
>
> *Me: You not gonna tell me?*
>
> *Jerry: Georgia.*
>
> *Georgia? Matteo in Georgia?*
>
> *Jerry: You know you owe me now.*
>
> *Me: What?*
>
> *Jerry: Come to the house.*

I knew I should have waited to text him. Sometimes Jerry was so… ugh.

> *Me: OMW*

Matteo

"Damn, I needed that nap." I yawned, looking around at my surroundings. The sun was peeking from behind mountains on my left side, and all I saw was trucks flying down the expressway. I wasn't used to this country shit. "Where we at?"

"That sign back there said we about 135 miles from Atlanta." Reno yawned himself. "I'm hungry like a muthafucka, let's go to Waffle House."

"What you know about Waffle House?" I tried stretching in the back seat before I gave up. "Pull over, I gotta get out."

"I don't know nothing 'bout Waffle House, but I need some food and I gotta piss," Reno replied. "It's a rest stop up here, I'll go there. I ain't trying to get hit by these trucks and be another dead nigga down here on the side of the road."

"Facts." We rode to the rest stop and parked. I hopped out first to stretch my legs. "We gotta get a hotel or something, I smell like yesterday."

"Yeah, and you got ya brother's brains on ya shirt too," he pointed out. "We should've changed clothes, that's why these people looking at us all crazy."

"Fuck these people, they act like they ain't never seen a killer in real life." I pulled my black tee over my head, yanking it off quickly. "My shirt black, so how they know it got blood on it?"

"Blood is thick and it sticks to cotton, jerk. Should've stopped last night and stretched." Reno chastised me a little as he passed me a clean tee from a new pack. "I stopped off at a twenty-four hour Walmart in Lexington while you was sleep and got us these."

I snatched the shirt from his hand and stretched the neck to give me a little extra room. "Pass me my phone, jerk." Reno tossed my iPhone in the air, and I caught it before it hit the ground. "See if you broke my shit, you'd be paying for it. You are my keeper, right?"

"I ain't Luca. Buy yo' own phone, ol' big-headed ass!"

"Fuck you, jerk." I teased, missing the times when me and both of my brothers talked shit to one another. Unlocking my phone as I walked inside the small building to piss, HER text stood out over all the bullshit, so I hit that one first. Until I saw her face, nothing else mattered to me. "A voice message?" I stopped walking and put the phone on speaker as I heard her words flowing from those lips, glad she was ok for the time being. "On her way to Georgia... cramping? We was just at the... wait, why she keep calling me Dr. Wu? Lemme think… lemme think… doctor… fix? Nah, she know I'ma take care of these niggas. Traveling… damn girl this ain't *Scooby Doo*! Reno!"

"What?"

"Here. Listen to wife message and tell me what she trying to say. I gotta piss." Tossing the phone at my brother, I headed inside the small building on the side of the road. After answering nature's call, I cupped a hand in front of my face to make sure I wasn't burning nobody's skin when I talked. "You need to get to a hotel before you go pick her up, nigga." I snickered at my reflection. "She definitely clowning if she smell that shit!"

I ran my hands under the faucet and wet my face, hoping the water wasn't from the creek or a well behind the rest area. Pushing a kid out of my way, I walked out the bathroom with a little energy, but not much. Yesterday was beginning to catch up with me, but I knew if I went to lay it down, I wouldn't be able to sleep because she wasn't next to me. "Reno! What she say!"

"You got a tracking app on ya phone?"

"Yeah... shit, you a muthafuckin' genius, Reno!" I snatched my phone from his hand and pulled up the FindMy app she made me install. Since her clinic was in the hood, Sommer said she was sharing her location with me so I'd be able to find her as long as she had her phone. As soon as I opened it, the app showed her exact location. "Apple found my baby. Sommer, I'm on my way."

§

We grabbed some clothes from the mall, which I hated shopping at, and checked into the Grand Hyatt. After a shower to wash Luca's blood off of me completely, I took care of my hygiene so I was back feeling like Matteo Marino. Soon as Reno finished getting ready, we pulled Sommer up on the app to see where we were going. "Decatur? Ain't that some shit."

"Well, your brother did say she was in Georgia." Reno chuckled, patting his pockets for the room key card. "Aye, what you got in the trunk?"

"Come on Reno, you know me," I scoffed. "These country niggas don't want this smoke."

"Shiiiit, kidnapping sis... yes they do." Me and my brother stepped in the elevator at the same time. Two chicks were in the elevator already molesting my brother with their stares. The situation didn't get any better when they noticed me standing behind him.

"Hey," the friendly one spoke up first as the second one raped a lollipop with her mouth. "Where y'all goin'?

"Why? You tryin' to do somethin' wit' them lips? Reno cornered them both as I hit the emergency stop button.

Second chick didn't say a word; she just dropped to her knees and hooked my brother up. "I'm good." I held a hand up when the first chick headed in my direction. "Wifey would kill me."

"What she don't know won't hurt her though. Anything that happens in this elevator, stays in this elevator," she cooed, rubbing her hand down my chest.

"Bitch, I said no. Go help ya' friend suck my brother up."

I lit up a cigar and watched for a minute, snickering at her for taking my advice before the elevator phone rang. "Yeah?" Reno answered the phone while lil' thotiana gagged on his meat.

"Sir, are you ok? Does anyone need medical assistance?" a voice questioned.

"Mmhmm." He put his hand over the phone's speaker to direct his personal show. "Lick under… right there." Reno moved his hand from the speaker to finish his conversation. "Nah, these hoes in the elevator sucking my dick."

"Tell 'em thanks for the southern hospitality." I chuckled with my phone on record. He was gonna want to remember this moment.

"Y'all heard my brother. We'll be down there in… shit, girl!" He gripped the wall and I busted out laughing as all sorts of shit dribbled from the girl's mouth. "You sure you straight, bruh? This girl neck game is A1!"

"I'm sure." I hit the button to restart the elevator as the second chick passed her friend a wet wipe from her purse. "Y'all some hoes, ain't y'all?"

"I ain't no hoe," the nasty one started first. "When I see something I like, I go get it."

"Oh, that's what they calling it now, huh." I sneered before my little brother stepped in.

"Aye, let's hook up later, aight? I wanna see you one more time before we go back up top." Reno stroked her face gently.

"Ok," she cheesed, exchanging numbers with my little brother just as the elevator stopped.

"Aye, make sure you answer that phone," he called out, balling his lip up and smacking her on all that ass. "Matteo, we gotta add a couple more days on the room. You saw shawty an' nem hook me up right there in the spizzot?"

"Reno, focus. We here for Sommer, aight?"

"I'm coming back out here. Man, I love Atlanta already." He popped the lift gate on the back of my truck, checking under the spare tire for the big boy artillery.

We climbed in the truck and hit the streets, pulling up to the address where Sommer's phone was pinging on the app. I already had the Glock on me, if I needed anything else Reno had it ready. Sommer's phone was pinging at a house in a neighborhood with four other houses on the whole block, all spread out with big lots between them. I parked on the street in front of the house and walked past the black Riviera to the front door and rang the bell. An older lady answered with a polite smile, wiping her hands on her apron.

"Hey, can I help you?"

"Yes, I'm looking for my wife, Sommer?" I questioned, squinting at the afternoon sun while I rubbed a hand over my waves.

"I don't want no trouble." A frightened looked settled over her face, and I saw her shiver slightly in the doorway.

"Oh, no trouble. Just here for my wife and I'll be on my way."

"What makes you think your wife is here?"

"Ma'am." I decided to speak to her like I would talk to my grandmother if she was still here. "You ever been married?"

"I have. My husband died three years ago." She looked off in the distance as the memories of her life as somebody's wife no doubt flooded her brain.

"As a married woman, was it the kids, your first house, or the Benz in the driveway that made you love him? Or was it him remembering your favorite soap, you coming home from a long day at work to a home cooked meal he made for you, or getting that 'I love you' text from him when it seemed like everything was going wrong... you know, the little things your husband did for you were what you cherished the most. Am I right?"

"Mmm...yes lawd," a small smile tugged at her lips as she heard me out.

"When it comes to my wife, I know that feeling. I miss holding her hand while I'm driving. I miss smelling her hair. I miss putting my hand over her heart while she asleep and realizing that mine beats the same as hers. I been up for the past twenty-four hours because she not next to me. I ain't here to start no trouble, and I appreciate you letting me come to you as a man. Real talk, I just want her back. That's all."

She pulled me in for a tight hug, patting my back like my auntie used to when I was a kid. "I can't let you go another minute without your wife, son. Sommer! Baby, your husband is here!"

Heavy footsteps inside the house hit the hardwood floors methodically behind her. A hand appeared and wrapped around her mouth dragging her body backward before the door slammed in my face. *These niggas serious, huh. Good. Me too.*

"Reno!"

"What's good, bro?"

"Aye, bring me the widow maker."

Reno ducked inside the car and came back with my AR-15 rifle already loaded. "Aye, if they did something to sis, don't forget you got the 4th of July under the third row."

"I gotta see her face. If they tell me she ain't here, then we can make some shit go boom, aight?"

"Gotcha, bro."

Dropping the first hollow point in the chamber, I aimed at the front window and started tugging at the trigger. Glass exploded in waves as the window rained tiny slivers throughout the flower bushes in front of the modest house. Pieces of brick ricocheted in clumps on the dirt beneath the bushes, removed in patches from the home's façade.

"AYE, MY MAMA IN HERE!" a voice yelled out from inside.

"Now that I have your attention, I'm gonna say it again. GIVE ME MY MUTHAFUCKIN' WIFE, MY NIGGA!"

"Who is yo' wife?" a younger feminine voice called out over the tinkering of shards falling from the window pane.

"SOMMER! IF YOU IN THERE, LET'S GO!"

"MATTEO! THEY SAID I CAN'T LEAVE UNTIL YOU GIVE THEM THEY MONEY!" Hearing her scared voice had me on go. I climbed in the window with Reno behind me, both of us with guns in hand.

"SOMMER!"

Reno's footsteps behind me stopped and I turned to see this nigga Nezz with a gun to my little brother's head. "Matteo. You in here shootin' up my mama crib?"

"MATTEO! THEY GOT A GUN TO MY HEAD, THIS GIRL GONNA KILL ME! BABY PLEASE GIVE THEM WHAT THEY WANT!"

"Nigga, that's my girl. I know you didn't think I was just gonna let you snatch her up and not come looking for her, did you?"

"Yo' brother said she was his. That's why we got her! She ain't going nowhere until I get my money!"

"How much Luca owe you?"

"A hundred and three thousand dollars, nigga!"

Three? These niggas don't do round numbers? "You gotta let my little brother go, he got the money." Reno and I exchanged glances, he knew what to do.

"Nah, three Marinos instead of two? Your woman, your baby, *and* your brother? I think the price just went up," the nigga that be with Nezz called out from behind me.

This nigga just threatened my whole family, and I wasn't about to take this shit lightly. "How much."

"Three hundred thousand sounds good to me. What about you, Nezz?"

"Three hundred sounds good, but a half a million sounds better." Nezz sucked his teeth, pushing my brother in my direction. "Put the guns down."

We dropped our weapons, and Nezz's weak ass friend came and patted us down. "I'ma ask you the same thing I asked your brother. For your sake I hope your answer ain't the same as his was. You got my money?"

"Aye, I got it. I was just about to go meet my folks when I got the call, so y'all can have that." I spoke sincerely. "It's in the truck."

"Go get it. Nah, you know what? We'll all go get it," Nezz insisted, signaling for his boy to follow us out to my truck.

"Reno, gimme the keys. That bag still in that one spot?"

"Yeah."

"Bet." The three of us walked to the truck, and they stood next to each other with guns trained on me as I popped the lift gate and moved the carpet to the side. While they were watching me, Reno crept backwards from where we were and headed inside. After shifting the spare tire back and forth a few times to make it seem like I was actually looking for this 'bag', I grabbed the pistol and fired two shots in both men before they realized what was going on. Stepping over their dead bodies, I smirked to myself, knowing what was going on inside the house before a second set of gunshots went off.

"SOMMER!"

"Matteo, take yo' sensitive ass on somewhere, you know I ain't let nobody hurt lil' sis," Reno called out as Sommer ran from a back room, crashing into my arms.

"I was so scared, Matteo! I was so scared!" her face was wet against my neck. "They were cool until we got here, that's when they started acting crazy! That girl pointed a gun at my stomach and said she was gonna…"

"Shhh… it's over, baby. It's over, ok?"

"Did you get my message?"

"Yeah. Reno had to figure it out, you know I don't be doing all that Inspector Gadget shit."

"Thanks, brother-in-law," she glanced over at Reno with an appreciative smile before turning back to me, running her hand down my cheek. "Baby, you look tired, when is the last time you got some sleep?"

"When I woke up yesterday next to you, pretty girl." I ran a hand through her hair like I always did when I hadn't seen her in a few hours. "We got a room at the Grand Hyatt in Buckhead. Let's go get some sleep."

"Right behind you, love. Reno, you coming?"

"I'll ride back to the spot with y'all, but I'ma have to take a raincheck. Bout to see what my new friends up to," he cheesed slyly. "Call me in the morning."

"Y'all killed that man mama too?"

Sommer stopped and gave me a deer-in-headlights look. I didn't wanna laugh, but that shit was funny. "Uhmm… Reno?"

"Yes, I put a bullet in mama's head too," he spoke firmly. "That's her kid, therefore a product of her creation. If she wasn't making people with them fucked-up attitudes, she would've been good. You don't bring the game to where yo mama stay, anything might happen."

Reno

Big bro and lil' sis needed their space, so I got my own room at the Intercontinental across the street while they slept. I called ol' girl who took care of me earlier, and she came back with the same friend. Oh my God, these ATL thots wasn't no joke! One of 'em even licked my ass. I wasn't expecting that, but I can't say I didn't like it. I didn't ask, and she didn't forewarn me, but the shit felt good.

The sun was way past early morning when I opened my eyes in the luxury hotel room. My text ringer went off and I pushed thot number one's head off my morning wood to check my messages. "Move bitch, I gotta go."

"Hmm… Craig, I thought you said we was going to breakfast at that one place?"

thot number two questioned. Breakfast? They didn't even know my real name.

"Y'all need an Uber or something?" I headed to the bathroom with my wallet and pistol to take care of my hygiene.

"Wait… you not taking us home?"

"No. I didn't pick you up, did I?"

"Aw, *hell* naw!" one of them screamed from inside the room. "Hell naw! Craig, you told us last night you 'had' us! Now we can't even get a meal?"

"What? You bitches hungry? It ain't eleven o'clock yet, if you hurry you can still get a carton of orange juice and a muffin from the continental breakfast." I smirked, walking out the bathroom. "Might even be able to still get one of those small boxes of Frosted Flakes. 'That one place' is downstairs in the lobby."

"You ain't shit, Craig!" Thot number two snatched their clothes from around the room, hopping on one foot as she pulled her leggings back on. "Come on, girl! Let's go!"

"I ain't shit, but both of y'all sucked my dick in the elevator while my brother watched, and you licked my ass. Y'all ain't known me twenty-four hours, but *I'm* the one who ain't shit? Y'all some comedians, for real."

Thot number one turned bright red with embarrassment as thot number two picked up the lamp from the table and tried to throw it at me, dropping it on the floor instead. "We the comedians, but you fucked both of us without a condom. How you know we ain't got herpes?"

"Or maybe we men too. This is Atlanta," thot number one added, smiling brightly.

"I ain't trying to hear that shit. I know fake titties when I feel them, and if one of y'all gave me anything, I'll be back. I know where you hoes live."

"How you know—"

I was sick of playing with two bitches whose time with me ran out when the sun came up. These hoes were overstaying their welcome. "Know what's funny? I ain't said nothing bout where I live. For all y'all know that man with me wasn't my brother, and I could live right around the corner! Guess we both gotta find out on our own, huh!"

They rushed out the room together, slamming the door behind them. Going back to my phone, I pulled up Tamra's message and reread it for a second time before I responded:

> *T: Reno, I'm so confused. X rubs my belly every morning before he leaves, and every morning, I wish more and more that it's your touch.*
>
> *Me: I know, T. I miss you and lil' man too. What you wanna do?*

T: We can't keep doing this. X deserves to know. He's a good man.

Me: I ain't tryna put you in a position where you may have to defend yourself and I'm not there. You still carrying my baby.

T: Come pick me up.

Me: Can't. I'm in ATL.

T: ATL? I WANTED TO GO!

Me: Lol, me and Matteo came down here on business.

T: When you coming home?

Me: Come out here.

T: Boy, you crazy. X will kill me.

Me: And I'll kill him.

T: Gotta go. Love you.

Me: Love you more.

It was crazy how me and Tamra hooked up at the comedy club. I was there meeting a client with one of the women who worked for me, and she was there with none other than Xander. Matteo called him to make a run, so he left Tamra with us. Not too long after, Lynise's date showed up and she was gone, leaving me and Tamra at the table together. Dave Chappelle showed up that night and shut the whole spot down; me and her kept retelling his jokes to one another long after he left.

Instead of me dropping her back off at home, we rode around for a while talking about life. I didn't open all the way up to her about my past, but there were some things I shared that my brothers didn't even know. In turn, she told me about her life as a porcelain doll for the city's second-in-command. Before X would leave for the day, he'd drop her off promptly at Luca's, then either send a Lyft for her or come pick her up himself. She wasn't allowed to go anywhere without checking in first. He claimed it was because he needed to know she was safe. According to Tamra, he wanted to keep her so safe she was beginning to question their whole relationship and whether or not she should be in it. I still remember the look on her face as she explained what a day in her world was like:

"Do you have someone, Reno?"

"Not really. I can get pussy if I needed it, but for the time being, I'm good."

"Well, hypothetically speaking, if you did have someone, would you make her stay in the house 24/7, only place she allowed to go is to work for your boss's brother?"

"Luca tried—"

"No, Luca treats me like his sister," she interrupted. *"What I'm saying is how do you feel about a woman having the freedom to come and go as she pleases?"*

"Well, I don't comment on the next man's relationship, but if the woman was mine, she

could do whatever she want. She grown. I know me, she'll be back."

"How you know?" She showed all thirty-two of her teeth in my direction with a curious gleam in her eye.

"That ain't yo' business but know that I know." I smirked in her direction.

"Reno, can I be honest with you?"

"Always keep it a buck with me, T. What's on your mind?"

"I used to have the biggest crush on you when I was in high school," she giggled shyly, lowering her head a little.

"Crazy thing is, I guess you can say I had a crush on you too when you was in high school. I didn't come at you because I knew how you were about X." I admitted, snickering more to myself than her.

"Why are you single, Reno? Do you not see yourself with anyone or is it that you

don't want to be with anyone?" she
questioned honestly.

"Real talk, I always said if I was gonna
do it, I was gonna do it right."
"What's 'it'?"
"Wife, kids, home… all that stuff. I never
wanted to be a serial dater or have women
running in and out of my life like that. The
woman I ultimately gave my time to would
be the woman I would always give my time
to. She deserved that and more from me if I
was asking her to give me her love, trust,
and soul."

"And have you found her?"
"I thought I did back in the day, but—"
"But what?"
"Then she started kicking it with Xander,
and I was back to the drawing board." I
divulged after all these years. Tamra
blushed before she turned away from my

serious glance. She asked and I spoke my truth.

I was always in love with Tamra. I was drawn to her beautiful soul before I was attracted to her beautiful flesh, and by the time I decided to shoot my shot, Xander already swept her off her feet. I was happy for Matteo's people, but in my eyes, he had my woman. Even then, I didn't take the Luca route.

"Xander is suffocating me. I don't hate him; I just wanna be happy for a few hours…" she spoke out of nowhere. "Is it wrong for me to get some air for a while?"

"Tamra, I told you before, I'm not the relationship whisperer. What I will say is that you grown. If you not happy, do something about it. Make yourself happy. He'll see it and either get on board or get left. Simple as that."

She gazed sincerely in my direction and I can't lie, her eyes made me wonder what was going on behind her comforting, brown orbs. "That simple, huh?"

"Yeah—mmm…" Tamra leaned over the arm rest and slipped her tongue in my mouth. Instinctively, I gripped the back of her neck in case she changed her mind. "You sure you wanna do this?" I questioned when we came up for air.

"Just for a little while, ok?"

"Come to my house."

"Does Xander know where you live?"

I didn't care about how Xander felt. If he pulled up to the spot, that was it, Tamra was more of my main focus than anything. "Turn off your phone."

She did as I asked, and I did something that night I'd never done with any other woman: I made love to her. When we got to my house, I carried her upstairs and laid her

*down on my bed. Her body was nothing
short of a work of art spread across my dark
gray comforter. I kissed her everywhere
from the top of her head down to her ankles,
then back up to French kiss her damp
mound. I slipped inside of her gently and
asked if she was ok while we shared each
other. We were so caught up in the moment
by the time we realized we hadn't used any
protection is when I was emptying my seed
deep in the cradle of her creation.*

I knew she was pregnant by me because
Matteo and Xander went down to the DR for
a few weeks to iron out a better deal on the
dope. Tamra spent those three weeks at my
spot, and when Matteo called to let me know
they were on their way home, I dropped her
back off at her place. A few weeks later, she
called and said not only had she missed her
period, but the last time she and Xander had
been together was a few weeks before her

regular cycle last month. Xander thought the baby was his, but after I took her to her first ultrasound, she knew the baby belonged to me.

And now, here we were six months later.

Sommer

Seeing Matteo and Reno show up to that house down in Atlanta was nothing short of a gift from God. After they saved me, Reno dropped us off at the hotel and went on about his business while Matteo and I got some much needed rest. I hadn't realized we slept the rest of the day and all of the night away until we woke up with the sun peeking over the horizon.

"Mmm… you ok, love?" he questioned as I stretched myself awake. "How's my baby?"

"We're fine." I smiled at the touch of his hand rotating in circles around my small belly. "How are you?"

"Better now that I got you back." Matteo pecked me on the cheek before getting up to go take care of his hygiene. "Did you get your vitamins while we were at CVS?"

"Hadn't planned on grabbing those, but can you grab me some for now? I'll get some better ones once we get home."

"Don't worry about the prescription. I want you to get them from Dr. Sebi's website. Not trying to expose my baby to all those fillers and chemicals they be putting in these vitamin supplements nowadays."

"Oh yea, I read about him. The herbalist, right?"

"Yea, Reno was telling us about him when he started his workout regimen. Switched his morning routine up after he got some stuff off the website, said his whole body feels like somebody cleaned up his organs. People out here making it seem like that man a fraud, but he knew something."

"True."

"And you a doctor, yet you agree."

"I mean…I'm not saying he curing EVERYTHING, but I do agree with people of color eating a balanced meal that isn't loaded down with fillers, sugar, and carbohydrates, that's all."

"So you'll check out his site?"

"I already ordered my prenatal vitamins from him, sir. Now if you don't mind, please go to the store and get me something off the shelf until my package comes. Please Matteo?"

"You ain't neva gotta beg me for nothing, cause I'm all in," he leaned over and kissed my cheek. "That king you carrying is always gonna be my first priority."

"Matteo, I told you I'm carrying a queen."

"Wanna bet? I got half a million dollars that say I'm right."

"I got half of ten dollars that say you wrong." I returned his cheek peck before going to take care of my own hygiene.

"I want my money in the delivery room, too. Don't be trying to renege!" he called out from the other side of the closed door.

"Boy, you are so crazy! Did you get my phone?"

"Where's your phone?"

I opened the door to the bathroom and stood in the doorway staring at him. "It was in the glove box inside the black Riviera."

"Naw, I didn't know it was in there."

"You think—"

"Hurry up and get dressed, baby." Matteo grabbed his phone and dialed a number putting it on speaker. Whoever he was calling didn't pick up, so he called three more times with the same response. "Where's the remote to the TV?"

"Right here." I passed it to him after I pulled my dress on. "Matteo, what's wrong?"

He tapped the power button on the remote and scrolled quickly through the channels. "I just hope these people—"

"We interrupt your regularly scheduled programming to bring you this breaking news from out of Decatur. A local resident discovered an entire family murdered in their home early Sunday morning. Police have no leads and no witnesses, but the local resident who found the bodies had this to say:"

"We's a peaceful people round here, know what I'm talmbout? This a peaceful neighborhood. Ms. Hattie Mae ain't never had nothing but a kind word for everybody she ever knowed, know what I'm talmbout? E'rybody loved Ms. Hattie Mae. Whoever did this to these nice folk ain't nothin' but the devil, you heard me? I say nothing but the damn devil!"

"Reporting live from Decatur, I'm Jovita Moore with Channel 2 Action News. Back to you in the studio."

"Baby, we gotta go before they find your phone. I ain't come all the way out here for you to be sitting in no Georgia jailhouse for questioning, and I ain't trying to be locked up in nan' either."

"Where's Reno?"

"Reno can take care of himself." He shot a quick text no doubt to his brother before he checked the room one last time for our stuff. "We should have just burned that house down. Shit!" he grumbled more to himself than me.

"I'm ready."

"Aight, babe. Let's go."

Keedra

"Breaking news out of Racine County: body parts of what appears to be an unidentified male washed up on the south shore of Lake Michigan today. Sources from the scene tell Fox 6 News that it appears the victim died from a single gunshot wound to the head. Police are asking anyone with information on this heinous crime contact the Racine Police Department at 262-886-2300. Back to you in the studio."

Jerry gave me some money to get my own place once he saw the bruise on my back from my mother's doing, and I was seriously thinking about taking his advice. I didn't need to be in the house with her. Even now, with me sitting in the living room watching the news, she was staring at me out the corner of her eyes with her nose turned up.

"Keedra."

"Yes, Mama?"

"You ain't take out the trash last night," she sucked her teeth, rolling her eyes at me.

"Wasn't no trash in the garbage when I left last night, Mama."

"Well, it is now. How you think it got there?"

I took a deep breath in and blew it out slowly counting to ten. "Mama, I don't know."

Before I knew it, she grabbed my ear and pulled me off the couch toward the kitchen. "You disrespectful as shit, Keedra! Look in this can! Look at it! See all that trash, Keedra! See that shit! That's what you left in this kitchen to funk my house up! I came down here this morning and the whole kitchen smelled like trash!"

"Mama it ain't nothing but two candy wrappers in here!" I yelled out, teetering over the small can. She had a firm grip on my ear, twisting it back and forth. "Let me go, dammit!" I tried to pry her hands off me.

I was caught completely off guard when her hand came up from nowhere and whacked my face. "The fuck you think you talking to, bitch! Yo' lazy ass gotta go! You ain't 'bout to be in my house sleeping all day and out all night while I'm at work, plus keep this house clean behind you! I don't care about you not having nowhere to go! Get the fuck out, Keedra!" My own mother pushed me to the floor as if I was some random in the street.

I got up and stood face to face with her, sick of her accusations about what I wasn't doing, knowing I was breaking my back to do everything she wanted before she asked so I didn't have to hear her mouth. "What have I ever done to you?" My mother had her days, but it seemed like the older I got, the more vindictive she became. "You gave birth to me, so I don't understand why you hate me so much!"

"I hate you because you EXIST! I never wanted you, Keedra! I only had you because your father was married and his wife told him she wasn't having no more kids after she gave him a son. He stopped giving me money for you when you were a baby because his wife found out about us and threatened to leave. All that shit he talked about how much he loved me... hmph! Love didn't make him stay either! I tried giving you to the state, but they said they would put me in jail for neglect, so I kept you! I begged your father to take you at least for a couple of months, but he said no! I hate Jerry for what he did to me!" she spat through gritted teeth.

I started heading towards the steps after she admitted to hating me but froze mid step because I couldn't have possibly heard her correctly. "Jerry? Mama, I thought you said my father's name was James?" A loud thumping noise started beating inside my head watching the corners of her lips purse together.

"James was the man I was fucking when you was a toddler. He was taking care of us, why wouldn't you call him daddy? Keedra, have you looked at your birth certificate?" Per usual, she felt the need to throw jabs when all I asked was a simple question.

"Mama, ain't nobody listed on my birth certificate as my father! Who is Jerry?"

"Hmph! Just because we wasn't married don't make him no less yo' real daddy." She sucked her teeth and turned her nose up again. "Your real father is Jerry Pembrooke, owner of the—"

"JERRY PEMBROOKE! Mama, I—oh my God. OH MY GOD!"

"Oh your God what, Keedra? Don't be trying to go up to his job and ask for no money! He gonna tell you no! I already tried it, for your information!"

"Did—Mama, how you know Jerry Pembrooke is my father? Did—did you do a DNA? Mama, how do you know!"

"I know because I know where my pussy been!" she screamed across the room to where I stood two seconds from fainting. "Plus, the asshole made me do a DNA, that's how I know!"

"I gotta—I gotta get out of this house…" I grabbed the railing for support; my legs felt wobbly trying to process what I'd been told. "I-I can't…"

"That's what I been telling you this whole time! Get out my house!" she yelled out.

Instead of going upstairs, I ran downstairs and snatched my keys from the fireplace. "Mama I can't believe—" I started then stopped. She wasn't gonna tell me what I needed to know. Nobody would. Nobody but somebody who was there…*somebody bout to give me some answers,* I thought, bursting through the front door. Running to my car, I couldn't get the key in the door fast enough; I had to get away from my mother and her…accusations? Lies? Or dare I say…truths.

This whole time… all the things we've done… this whole time… I started out having sex with my brother, then graduated to my own father? My stomach rumbled a second before everything I'd ate in the past twenty-four hours spewed from my lips.

"Don't leave that in front of my house, girl! Getcho ass back here!" her voice hollered from the porch as I hopped in my vehicle and sped off down the street.

§

Driving 90 mph to get to Jerry's condo, my mother's words played in a fractured loop over and over in my head. *Your real father is Jerry Pembrooke... Your real father is Jerry Pembrooke... Your real father is Jerry Pembrooke...* My real father had been...oh my God. The thought alone had me dry heaving on the side of the road for the second time that day. I couldn't believe I never noticed the resemblance between me and him. Why do people keep secrets like this from their families? Why didn't I know about this before now? Why am I throwing up all over... oh my God... *we never... what if... what if I'm... he never wore a fucking condom... Jerry said he had a vasectomy... oh my God...*

"Jerry!" I hopped out the car with the ignition still on and ran to his townhouse. "Open this door, dammit! JERRY!"

"Shhh... Keedra, what is wrong with you?" The door opened and he nudged me away, shushing me in the process. "My wife is here and she's sleeping. What's so important you had to come over here now?"

"Your wife is here? Oh, lemme come in so we can have this conversation as a family then!" I shoved him out the way, barging inside.

"Keedra, what are you—oh yeah." He stopped and covered his mouth as we both heard rustling from upstairs. "You're... damn, what was her name?"

"Kiana." I was stunned at the fact he didn't even remember my mother's name, considering they had a child together.

"Kiana's daughter. Yeah. I got that pussy young, did she tell you I was her first?" he snickered contemptuously, but I didn't find it funny. Now it made sense why my mother was so upset he didn't want her. But she had me the day after her sixteenth birthday...

"Jerry, I miss you," a woman's voice sang from the steps. "Who was at the— Keedra?"

"Sheena? Really?"

"Go back upstairs while I take care of this situation, ok?" he soothed, kissing her cheek while patting her ass. Sheena and I exchanged glares before she walked slowly back up the steps with a small smile on her face. *Jealous bitch. Can't keep her legs closed for shit.* "Keedra, how was I supposed to know—"

"Maybe if you'd been in my life, you'd know who I was!" I shot back, feelings of shame and embarrassment flooded my soul. "Do you know what we've done, Jerry? What I've done with my own brother!"

"You got some good pussy too, just like your mother did," he moved closer, caressing my face with the back of his hand.

"JERRY!"

"Ain't nothing we can do about it now, the damage has been done, right?" he moved closer still, lips hovering just outside of mine. "Why you making such a big deal about it?"

"Why am I making such—ARE YOU SERIOUS!"

"All it means is every time you called me daddy, you weren't just playing a role. Now I know you care about me."

I backed away from where he stood before I strangled him dead. "Oh my God... Jerry, I can't believe..."

"You can't say I ain't never took care of you. I been giving you money for the last five years," his face contorted into a blur; I saw his teeth grinning like a Cheshire cat with his voice echoing in my ears. "Nobody has to know but me and you. We don't have to talk about this ever again, sweetie. Let's put this small faux pas behind us."

"Faux pas? Is that what I am to you? A faux pas?" I whispered, head still pounding. Only now it was creeping up my neck.

"Keedra—" The last thing I saw before I fainted was his hands reaching out. I prayed I'd hit the floor and crack my skull open before I allowed Jerry to put hands on me again.

Matteo

I'd been lying low since we had to get the fuck out of Atlanta a few months ago. Sommer was getting bigger by the day, and I loved every minute of it. We went to the ultrasound, and for an hour this baby showed us everything but whether he was a boy or girl. I knew then it was a boy; only a Marino man was that damn stubborn. Every day wife was texting me with something else crazy she had a craving for. It had gotten to the point I dropped her off at Reno's and gave him money to cook whatever she wanted. Her lil' fat butt was happy then.

Shannie's funeral was small; only me, the wife, and Reno were there for the service. Even still, I had her transported from the funeral home to her gravesite in a glass carriage pulled by two white Clydesdale horses with a black coachman dressed in all white. Never in the city's history did a crackhead have a bigger funeral procession than Shannie Tyler. People came out of their homes just to watch her casket move down the street. The whole hood came out and paid their final respects to my sister-in-law, as they should have.

Reno and Tamra were still sneaking around the city whenever they could. That night he told me about him getting her pregnant had me stuck because Xander treated that girl like she was Snow White and he was the only dwarf. She got a little freedom when she worked for Luca, but when that doctor said bed rest for a few weeks, he took that shit way too far. I think what they meant was that she couldn't be outside in that Milwaukee weather, but X said she was staying in the house until her due date.

Surprisingly, my brother allowed it. He didn't want her overly excited while she was pregnant. If I knew Reno, wasn't nobody or nothing stopping him from being in that delivery room when the time came. I was already looking through the team to see who could step into X's place once I dropped him in a patch of concrete in a few months.

Luca's body parts had been washing up on the lake for the past few weeks. They found his torso the other day. My people said they were still missing one of his legs, three of his fingers, and a hand. Reno filed a missing person's report the day he got back from Atlanta so we weren't implicated in his death.

The property management company contacted us to give their condolences and let us know his apartment was a crime scene, as if we didn't already know that.

Once the police gave the all clear, they'd call us back to clean his stuff out the spot.

Keedra called earlier saying we needed to talk, and I was ready to hear her out. I still hadn't found out who sent wife that message, but at this point, it didn't matter. Me and Sommer were in a good place in our relationship where she trusted me, and vice versa. I told Keedra to come by the house at two o'clock, that way I had time to run over to Reno's spot and pick the wife up. I didn't need no crossed lines, no insinuations, no messages, nothing. Sommer was petty as hell; I was still finding those screenshots in my closet a month later.

Jogging up the steps in front of Reno's house, I was just about to tap in the code when the door swung open. Sommer stood in the doorway with a sandwich in one hand and her purse in the other. "Hey, baby daddy. You ready?"

"Baby daddy, huh?" I leaned in and kissed her neck, checking out the outfit she had on. Sommer looked sexy as hell as always, dressed in an all-white, form-fitting dress that hugged her like a glove, showing off our baby bump. I'd just bought the gray Dolce and Gabbana leather biker jacket hanging around her shoulders while we were on our way back from Atlanta, only because she convinced me it matched her gray stilettos perfectly. Sommer knew I loved her hair straight down her back, and I promptly ran my fingers through her strands.

"I don't recall saying 'I do', so that makes you my baby daddy." She kissed my lips before heading for the truck. I ran ahead of her and grabbed her door, making sure she was comfortable.

"So I get yo' lil' dusty ass seven carats, and that don't mean shit, huh?" I hit the push button start and pulled out the driveway.

"Seven carats? This a cubic zirconia, boy what'chu talking about?" She raised her hand and wiggled her fingers while disconnecting my phone from the Bluetooth.

"This ain't." I reached in my pocket and passed her a ring box. Pulling over on the side of the road, I leaned over and wiped the tears streaming down her face. "Oh, now we quiet, huh?" I grinned, watching as her hand shook slightly.

"Matteo... you make me so sick." She opened the box slowly and got the shock of her life when she saw the new ring I got for her. "This is so beautiful, baby."

"Am I baby daddy, or am I baby? I'm confused, big mama." I took the box from her and took the ring out, sliding the deep blue sapphire set in a platinum band on top of the two carat white pear diamond I originally gave her when I proposed. My jeweler was out of town, and that was all I had access to at the moment.

"You baby. You my baby, Matteo," Sommer showered me with kisses before she tried to climb over the armrest, but Junior stopped all that. "I'll thank you when we get to the house," she purred, rubbing my mans through my jogging pants.

"Uhhh… about that. Sommer, I got something to tell you."

"Matteo, please. Can this wait? Lemme enjoy my new ring!"

"I came to pick you up because I don't want Keedra coming at you or sending nobody to come for you." I pulled back onto the street and headed home.

"Why would she do that?"

"Sommer, you know I love you, right?"

"Why would Keedra come for me, Matteo?"

"You uhmm…you remember back when we uhhh… when you went to the casino that one time?"

"Go on."

"Keedra, uhhh… baby, one day we gonna look back at this whole thing and laugh about it…"

"We ain't laughing about it today though. What did you do, Matteo?"

"I love you, Sommer. That ring alone should tell you how much I love you. We got a whole baby…"

"MATTEO WHAT DID YOU DO!"

"I swear I didn't do nothing, love. She, uhhh… she…"

I pulled up to the house not expecting to see her car parked in front of the gate, this bitch was fifteen minutes early. *Damn.*

Sommer's door swung open before mine, but she was stuck trying to fight the seat belt while wobbling out of the passenger side of the truck. "What is she doing here, Matteo!"

"Get back in the truck, Sommer! What if something happen to my baby!"

"*Your* baby?" Keedra wobbled out of the driver's side of her car. "What about *our* baby?" she proclaimed proudly, rubbing her small baby bump.

Sommer was walking to where we were, but stopped when she heard those words, staring back and forth between us with her mouth dropped open in shock. "Really, Matteo? REALLY, MATTEO! Now I know who sent that 'Congrats, step mama' bullshit!"

"Keedra, listen—" I put both arms out to hold both women at bay. From the frown on Sommer's face and the smirk on Keedra's, something told me this wasn't gonna go well.

"No, Matteo, *you* listen!" Keedra screamed. "You promised me the last night we made love you'd be there for me and our child! Now you got this bitch—"

"'Made love'?" I had to stop her right there. "We wasn't making love when you lived here, much less when you didn't! Aye, what the fuck you on, man?"

"Oh, now you don't remember?" she smiled slyly. "That day a few months ago when I came over to get my stuff? You told me you loved me! You promised you'd—"

"I told you—"

"Matteo Constantine Marino, what the hell is she talking about?" I ducked because I didn't know if Sommer was gonna take a swing at me behind my back.

"Constantine? Your middle name is Constantine?" Keedra pointed and laughed at me. "I know you half Italian, but damn!

Your mama should've fucked a black man because Constantine is NOT sexy!"

Before I could stop myself, I grabbed her neck and squeezed, slamming her body against the hood of the car. She could say what she wanted about me, but my mama was off limits, even if it was a weak ass jab. "What I tell you that day in the basement, Keedra? Huh? What the fuck did I tell you, Keedra!"

"Bitches... bitches bleed... Matteo, please..." she clawed desperately at her neck.

"Bitches bleed... finish it! Finish it, dammit!"

"Bitches bleed just like us..." she wheezed.

"I'll murder a pregnant hoe too. Don't forget that." I leaned down to whisper in her ear, finally releasing my grip. "Get the fuck outta here, Keedra."

"BYE KEEDRA!" Sommer picked up a brick from near the front gate and threw it at Keedra's head, connecting perfectly with the curve of her skull. "Matteo, let's go!"

I made sure Keedra made it back to her car; I might not have a relationship with her, but if she died that was another problem on my hands. My girl was a good girl, but carrying a Marino made that mean streak of hers even worse. "Go straight to the hospital. Call me so I know what's going on with you," I whispered quickly, kicking her car door.

"Oh, don't let me interrupt!" Sommer threw her hands up in the air and headed back to the truck, only this time she walked to the driver's side. "Y'all all in love, making kids, whispering I-love-yous! Everybody wanna play games, everybody wanna have an epiphany, everybody think it's cute to fuck with the doctor's head!"

"Sommer calm down—"

"I'm the one who needs to calm down, Matteo? ME? I'm confused on why I need to calm down when YOU'RE the one who stuck you dick in this...ugh, really? You leveled up only to go BACK to the trash?"

"Baby, I swear this wasn't supposed to happen. She sucked my—"

"Oouuu, that's all it takes? Suck on your lil' ding-a-ling and get a baby? Tuh!"

"You didn't have to, but we got one, don't we?" I shot back. Sommer wasn't 'bout to have me out here looking like the friendly neighborhood thot.

"Whatever you say, Matteo. Yea, I gotta go, apparently my presence isn't appreciated!"

Keedra was about to pull off, but rolled down the driver's side window and stuck her head out to stir up more bullshit. "It didn't take much, hoe! When a nigga love yo' pussy, it don't matter how much money you got or don't got, long as that kewchie still poppin'!"

Sommer looked at me with tears in her eyes and it wasn't nothing I could say to take that day a few months ago back. "Must be nice, huh. Got a doctor and a thot pregnant, best of both worlds, huh."

"Sommer, please—"

"I'm gonna go home for good this time." She took two steps backwards, palms facing outward each time I tried to comfort her. "Don't worry, I'll text when I'm in the hospital."

"She ain't...Sommer that ain't my baby!"

"I do have to thank you for showing me what love COULD be, though," she continued as a dark blue SUV sped towards us. "How a man COULD treat you, what the possibility of love MIGHT look like in a different lifetime under different circumstances. For that I thank you, Matteo."

"Sommer, let's just go in the house and talk—"

Even while trying her best, nothing she did stopped the tears spilling from her pretty brown orbs. "My Uber is here."

As she reached to open the door, I lunged forward, she wasn't leaving until I made this right. "Don't do this, Sommer. Please don't—"

Her hand…that delicate hand of hers smoothed over my chest many nights, rubbed my back when the world crumbled around me, soothed me on those days I wanted to blow everything up, fed me when I was hungry, bathed me and I felt safe, comforted me when I was about to spaz…that same hand palmed my face full of sorrow and regret. "Goodbye Matteo Constantine Marino. It was fun while it lasted, right?" she whispered, connecting soft lips to mine for the last time.

I wanted to pull her out of that back seat, carry her bridal style inside OUR home, and spend the rest of the night apologizing to her the right way. Sommer needed to know she was everything to me, our baby completed that bond. I didn't lie to her at my brother's house, I meant what I said when I told her I was her family. And now, watching the Uber turn around in my driveway, all I could do was watch her leave.

"Now that she's gone—"

Keedra.

KEEDRA.

"Didn't I tell you to get the fuck away from my house!" I roared, going for my pistol. THIS BITCH was the reason Sommer left. Now all I had was some funky ass memories, hoping she kept her word and called when she had my baby?

The squealing of Keedra's tires brought me out of my reverie, smoke from the raggedy muffler polluted the air once she finally got the hint.

I fucked up in the worst way possible. And now it was up to me to make it right between us for the sake of us being able to coparent. Fuck that, I want my baby back.

§

Make you do right
Love'll make you do wrong
Make you come home early
Make you stay out all night long

This thing with Sommer reminded me of late nights laying in bed as a kid listening to Al Green begging for forgiveness no doubt to the woman he was loving on at the time. Only it wasn't my mother playing old school music, usually it was my father. She was the one staying out late, sometimes all night while he sat home with me and my brothers, worried. But she came home. Every time. And every time, regardless of what she may or may not have been doing in the streets, he welcomed her back with open arms. I don't know if that was Auntie Kayla's life too, but her daughter wasn't having it.

Love is
Walking together
Talking together
Singing' together

I can't believe she got me over here sitting on the couch listening to some damn Al Green. Usually Sommer called when she made it home, but here it was three hours later and I hadn't heard anything from her. I reached for my phone to put it on do not disturb when I saw a text from a number not saved in my phone. I opened it up to read:

2627963798: CAT scan didn't show any damage. Doc said I had a bruise, but it wasn't too bad. They stitched my head and gave me some acetaminophen for pain because of the baby.

Me: Thought you wasn't pregnant.

2627963798: I am. X sent you the test.

Me: He said Nezz sent that from his phone.

2627963798: You saw me

Me: I'll pay this bill, but I ain't paying for no kid until I get a DNA. Hit the jack when you ready.

2627963798: I really need to talk to you, Matteo. It's important.

Me: About?

2627963798: Too much to text. Can I come over?

Me: I'll let you know.

Switching my phone to do not disturb, I headed upstairs to take a shower and go to bed. I knew the streets was poppin', but Sommer was mad. Streets didn't mean shit to me if she was gone, cause I definitely wasn't replacing her. Al helped me come up with a plan to fix it, and that's what I was gonna do first thing in the morning.

Sommer

"Sommer, it's going to be ok," Lana soothed in my ear. "I'm sure this Keedra person is lying."

"I shouldn't have said anything," I wept in my best friend's ear. "I should've went in the house and made him a bowl of cereal with a teaspoon of bleach," I sniffed.

"Sheesh Sommer, do you want the man emotionally hurt or physically dead?" she giggled.

"Lana, I thought I was happy. I thought we were good."

"Honey, you were good—"

"Then why would he risk us to be with a bar hopping hoe?"

"Sommer, I don't know. Sometimes men are just assholes, plain and simple. No rhyme or reason to it. You did the right thing, as women it's our job to love, honor, and respect our life partner. HOWEVER, never let them make you feel you're beneath them, because that's when they walk all over you."

I had to blow my nose from crying as she spoke. For the past three hours, all I'd been doing was crying; Matteo broke my heart. And while I was pregnant with his baby, no less. If there wasn't a small person involved who potentially looked like him, I could walk away clean, but finding out I was adopted, had an identical twin, and losing said twin all in the same year was incentive for me to carry this baby full term and figure out the rest later. "I changed who I was for him, Lana. Surprised you didn't see a video on TikTok of me beating on his ex when she came to his house that one time."

"Torrie is the TikTok junkie, remember? I hate social media." Lana seethed playfully. "Plus, we're talking about mental overload and adrenaline, you know that Dr. Park." I loved my friend; she always reminded me of who I was when I needed it the most. "Endorphins triggered your fight or flight response, next thing you know you're bashing someone's face in. Especially if you saw her as a threat."

"I did. But I'm trying to figure out if the threat was physical or mental."

"Sommer, you made the best decision you could with the information you had. Be gentle with yourself when you release any shame or guilt from that situation."

I took her words and used them to soothe the parts of my aching soul where Matteo took up space in my heart. "It just hurts so bad, seeing her get out of that car rubbing her baby bump and me not knowing they slept together recently. Why didn't he say something beforehand?"

Lana took a deep breath in and blew it out, choosing her words carefully. "Friend, I'm gonna say this to you and I need you to hear me clearly. Now I have yet to meet this Matteo person, but judging from our conversation now, and seeing you a couple times on FaceTime, I can say this with certainty."

"What's that?"

"Honey, you have a man in love with you who doesn't mind hurting people's feelings when it comes to you."

"What?"

"Apparently you didn't hear me so I'm gonna say it again. YOU HAVE A MAN IN LOVE WITH YOU WHO DOESN'T MIND HURTING PEOPLE'S FEELINGS WHEN IT COMES TO YOU. You said Matteo has kicked that Keedra person out of his house, choked her while she was pregnant, for which he could easily go to jail if she decided to press charges—"

"Which she ain't—"

"That's because apparently, she's delusional. Any rational woman would've been dialing 911 with one hand while screaming at the top of her lungs for the neighbors to call for help."

"True."

"He could've gotten some years behind that. But he didn't care. The man drove…not took a flight but DROVE here from your house because he had to come get his baby, and I ain't talking about the one you pregnant with. Yes, he may have been wrong to do what he did with that Keedra person, but I'm sure he has a reason why he did it. Anything other than him admitting he wants both of y'all I think warrants some forgiveness."

That whole Keedra thing was inevitable; deep down I knew her silence didn't necessarily equate to her moving on. "At least now I know who sent that sonogram."

"Didn't you say you spent some time at his brother's house? I'm sure he had an opinion on this Keedra person, whether good, bad, or indifferent."

"Honestly, based on everything Reno told me, I don't know what made her think she was pregnant by Matteo," I spoke my truth. Lana's words about Matteo not caring about anyone's feelings when it came to me hit home. Something he said after we got back from Atlanta popped up in my head for some reason:

"I got a reputation on these streets."

"A reputation? As what? Dr. Park's baby daddy?"

"Keep playing with me, Sommer." *Matteo bit my nipple, mashing his thick*

manhood against my middle. "I'ma give yo'
ass twins tonight."

"That's not how that works, Matteo.
That's not how any of that works." I mushed
his head before I stood up and headed for
the bathroom.

"Streets know me as a coldhearted goon,
but I wouldn't mind being known as Mr. Dr.
Parks. I love you, Sommer."

"I love you too, Mr. Dr. Parks," I
giggled before we shared a sloppy kiss,
which ended up us spending the rest of the
evening enjoying one another…

"Sommer?"

"I miss him, Lana. I miss him so much,"
The waterworks started fresh and anew once
more, Matteo was my heart. No amount of
dislike towards his ex would change US.

"He'll be back. I can guarantee that."

Reno

Tamra called and said she was having some cramping, so we had to go get that checked out ASAP. My baby boy had eight more weeks before he was due to make his entry in the world, and he needed to cook as long as possible. Tamra seemed a little depressed lately, if she wasn't going to her appointments X didn't want her going nowhere. She had to open the window to get some air, let him tell it. Doc was concerned because she wasn't getting enough exercise, but you think that nigga cared? Hell naw. So when I got word X was on the block, I went over his house and picked her up so she could do what she needed to do.

"Since you're around thirty-two weeks now, I believe the cramping you're experiencing is the normal stretching of your ligaments that women experience during their first pregnancy. You don't appear to be in active labor, just monitor your pain and come back if it worsens or you feel a sudden gush of liquid or see bleeding. However, Tamra, I'm looking over your blood work, and I gotta admit I'm worried about your eating habits. Are you getting enough iron in your meals?" Dr. Webster questioned, reviewing her chart.

"I eat, but I haven't been taking my prenatal vitamins as much as I should," she admitted sadly.

"Why not, dear?"

"My, uhmm… my boyfriend hasn't been able to get to CVS to pick them up for me."

"Mr. Marino—"

"Nah, Doc, she ain't talking about me." I nipped that in the bud quick; I ain't no deadbeat. "Now that I know she out, I'll take care of that pronto. She need to be making sure my baby got what he needs to grow."

"I didn't think you were aware," Doctor Webster nodded, reviewing her chart astutely. "But I also know Ms. Grant is in a situation, so I won't pry."

"Thank you." Tamra laid back on the exam table and lifted her shirt. Doctor Webster grabbed the Doppler ultrasound device and poured the gel on my baby mama's stomach. "Let's just make sure baby's heartbeat is strong, and then we can let you go home."

I loved hearing my baby's heartbeat. I would hear his little heart tones in my sleep for days afterward. As soon as she pressed the fetal stethoscope to her baby bump, and the familiar beat came through the small speaker, I knew something was wrong. "Doc, you hear that?"

"Yes, Mr. Marino, I do. Tamra, we're going to go ahead and admit you as a precautionary measure." Doctor Webster ducked out the room for a second, then returned with a nurse.

"Why? What's wrong—Reno?"

"I ain't no doctor, but his heartbeat sounds irregular to me." I sat her up to fluff her pillow before helping her lie back down. "How are things at home? X fucking with you still?"

She turned away, staring out the window with her lips pursed together. "Reno—"

The nurse hooked her up to the baby EKG and another machine that monitored her heart rate. I watched as Tamra's face frowned slightly when she quickly wrapped the Velcro and elastic belt around her to hold the baby Doppler still so it didn't slide off her round belly. Giving us both a tight smile, she nodded before she ducked out the room as quietly as she came in.

"I don't wanna hear that shit about how good of a man Xander is. I wanna know is he fucking with you?"

"Reno, I can't leave him—"

"You can't leave him? So you ok with him putting my baby at risk?" I tried hard not to raise my voice, but she wasn't making no sense. Fuck him, when it came to Reno Achilles Marino III I'd body his ass today if something happened to my son.

"You wouldn't understand, Reno," she dropped her head and wept. "We lost a baby before, and now I'm pregnant. He's looking out for my best interests by making sure I'm not in a position to lose this one."

"So that's why he locks you up in the house by yourself and says you can't leave? You can't go outside and get some air, you can't go to the corner and back? You can't even get the fucking mail?"

"I-I think he knows about us," she revealed.

"Why you say that?"

"I woke up one night to go to the bathroom, and he was staring me in the face with tears in his eyes. I asked him what was wrong, and he said… nothing."

"So?"

"Reno… Xander and I have been together since high school. I know this hurts him as much—"

"You know what? I ain't gonna make you choose between me and your high-school sweetheart. I will say this though: you and him ain't gonna be raising my son like he the one that's supposed to save y'all relationship. I'll be damned if I'm gonna stand by like some duck ass nigga and just say, 'Ok, baby. You and your man can raise my son.' You got me fucked all the way up if you think that's gonna happen; I'll walk in your house and take him if I have to!"

"Reno, I'm not saying that! I just need time—"

"How much more time you need, Tamra? You had thirty-two weeks to tell him about us!"

"Reno, he would've made me leave—"

"So? You act like I ain't got a six-bedroom, four bath house that I live in by myself! Man, save all them excuses and shit. This would've gone a lot different if you would've just got an abortion! I would've paid for that!"

"Reno, are you saying you don't want our baby?" Tamra all of a sudden cared about my seed, like she wasn't just pleading with me to understand how her man felt about me knocking her up.

"Tamra, I *never* said I didn't want our baby. I love my son, and I damn sure want him. I want his mama too. I want you to have the rest of my babies, I ain't trying to have all these different women out here with my kids! What I'm saying is that you want me to sympathize with the nigga that's stressing you out and gave my baby a fucking arrythmia in utero! If he don't make it, I ain't responsible for whatever actions I might take against ya man! Trust and believe that!"

"An arrythmia? In utero? Reno, you been watching *Grey's Anatomy* without me?" she snickered.

"Man, what I'm supposed to do at night? You got me hooked on that shit, y'all know I don't be in the streets." I cackled with her. "Tamra, all I'm saying is that you don't have to go through none of this. I wanna be the one waking up next to you and rubbing your belly. I wanna be the one you cuss out because you want something to eat every twenty minutes. I wanna know all ya crazy cravings. Matteo drop Sommer off at my house for days so I can cook for her. I wanna cook for you too… that way, I know both of my babies eating." I rubbed her ponytail while she blushed.

"I just feel like there's a sense of loyalty there between me and Xander that I don't want to break. He's been there for me for so many moments in my life that I feel like I owe him. Reno, we were wrong for doing what we did—"

"And still do. You left your panties at my house the other day."

"And did. I don't want no bitch laid up in my baby daddy bed," she tucked into her pillow comfortably.

"Bitches ain't allowed at my crib, so you good." I leaned in and kissed her pink lips. "I get that you and him have a past, and that's cool. But you ain't gonna never be happy if you base the future of your relationship on your past. What happened to the cool lil' chick who sat across from me that night and asked if it was ok for her to breathe? Is she still holding her breath?"

"She's breathing now, thanks to you," she smiled with her head bowed.

"That's all I'm saying. You want me to go talk to X? Tell him he ain't gonna be in the delivery room with my baby? Neither of y'all?""

"No, I'll tell him," Tamra spoke with renewed strength. "I hate to say it, but our relationship has run its course and we're both holding on to something that really isn't there anymore."

"Do I need to be there?" I didn't know if X ever put hands on Tamra, but I knew he was one of them niggas who couldn't keep their hands to themselves. He'd put hands on a few of my girls before that I had to get at him about.

"I'll be fine, Reno. I'll just let him know, and we'll move forward from there."

"Yeah, I need to know when this conversation is happening. Now before you say you got it, I'm telling you again: that nigga can't tell me nothing when it comes to you because you carrying my son. Matter of fact, I'ma call him up here right now." I texted X and told him to come to the hospital because I had something to tell him.

"Reno—no! Why would you do that?" Tamra sat up suddenly, anxiously wringing her hands. She seemed genuinely scared of what X was going to do if he found out.

"I know this nigga ain't hitting you, but what is he doing to you? Tell me, Tamra."

"Reno, he—"

"Aye, I was already in the area when I got ya message, chief." X walked calmly inside the room, looking back and forth between me and Tamra before resting his gaze on her. "What's going on?"

"Xander, I—" she trembled with her mouth stuck open as I texted Matteo.

"What have you done, Tamra? Hmm? Been hoeing around with these Marino niggas?" He sucked his teeth, focusing his stare on her neck.

"Look, X—" I began before he put his hand up to shush me. "Nigga, I ain't none of these hoes out here! You ain't 'bout to be hushing me! Tamra got something to tell you, I suggest you listen!" I looked at her lying on the bed as white as the sheets she was lying underneath when the nurse burst in the room.

"Everyone out now! Her heart rate is off the charts! We *have* to get this baby stable!"

"That's my baby mama! I ain't—" I yelled out as the nurse pushed *both* of us out of Tamra's room.

"Unless you're God, you, him, and nobody else is allowed in that room until that baby's heart rate returns to normal! Now, I don't know what the deal is between you two, nor do I care. But if your presence affects her mental state, it affects baby. If you haven't got the message, that means get the fuck out of this hospital until she calls you and tells you to come back, or I will have you both arrested for child endangerment. Are we clear?"

I looked Xander up and down, sucking my teeth before nodding. "Yeah, we clear. Ain't we, X?"

"Mmhmm," he sized me up for a few seconds before sucking his teeth at me. "We good."

"Now, Mr. Marino, you can take the first elevator, and Mr.… I'm sorry, who are you?"

"Laws. Xander Laws. That's my fiancée you got in that room, so you betta take care of her." X called himself threatening the same nurse who just threatened us. The same nurse who put us out for stressing out my son.

"Mr. Laws, you can take the second elevator."

"I ain't going no muthafuckin' where until I find out why I was called up here in the first place!" Xander roared.

"Nigga, you was already here, what you mean?" I walked up on him before the nurse put her arm out to stop us. "You know why you here!"

"Yolanda, call security. I'm not gonna play referee with these two when there's a baby whose life hangs in the balance!" she yelled out.

"His life?" I stopped, reality punching me in the gut as Xander swung on me…

Matteo

I don't know how long I was asleep, but a constant beeping was what woke me up. Even though my phone was on do not disturb, anyone on my favorites could still contact me with no problem; everyone else got the voicemail or hoped I responded to their text. My phone was downstairs, but the house was so quiet I still heard it loud and clear. Standing up to stretch, I went in the bathroom and swished some mouthwash to get the sleep taste out of my mouth before jogging downstairs to see what was up.

Scrolling through my texts, the plan was to see if there was anything from Sommer or my brother before I went back to see what the unsaved number in my phone wanted. It seemed as if the unsaved number's texts went on forever, so I took a few minutes to see what she wanted:

2627963798: Matteo, I know you said you'll let me know, but I just feel like we've been through too much to end like this.

2627963798: Yes, I might've jumped the gun on that whole proposal thing, but can you blame me? Matteo, you have been the key to my heart for the past five years now, and nothing? You put me out your house like I'm trash.

2627963798: That whole thing with Luca, I was drunk. He told me to come over, and we started drinking. One thing led to another, and the video happened. Your brother took advantage of me. Did he apologize to you for what he *did? I bet he didn't.*

2627963798: What can I do that will change your mind? I'll do anything.

*2627963798: Nobody loves me,
Matteo. Nobody. My mother told me
she hates me, and I found out Jerry
is my biological father.*

*2627963798: Matteo, please, call me
back. I love you. I love our baby. You
don't want Sommer. You want me. I
forgive you. Please, Matteo.*

*2627963798: I'm in that dark place,
Matteo. You remember, like I was
before. It's cold, Matteo. I'm
freezing.*

*2627963798: I'm sorry for
everything. I never meant to hurt you,
Matteo.*

*2627963798: Why are you treating
me like this? Does our baby really
not mean anything to you?*

2627963798: Matteo.

2627963798: Matteo, please

2627963798: I'm gonna keep texting until you answer me.

2627963798: MATTEO!

Ain't nothing sadder than a begging ass woman. I deleted her messages so I could see what was going on in the streets when Reno's text came through, saying Tamra was at the hospital, and X just walked in. Had to hit talk on that one immediately:

"Bro, what's going on?"

"I need you up here ASAP."

"On my way now." I hit end and started looking around for my keys when something told me to look at the text again. Squinting, I saw it was actually a group text with me, Sommer and Luca's number flashing on the screen. I knew if Luca showed up it would be some shit, considering I murked him a few months ago. Sommer got the text too, though? She loved her some Reno. Which meant I was gonna have time to plead my case after I bodied X for fucking with my little brother. Tonight 'bout to get interesting…

§

I got to the hospital and parked in the garage across the street. Sommer's little Nissan Altima pulled up behind me and she backed into the empty stall three spots down, wiping her eyes when she got out. I met her at the door, not wanting anything between me and her scent, her touch, her aura. I needed this woman. More than that, I needed her to know how much I needed her. "Aye."

She wiped her nose before taking a deep breath in and blowing it out, focusing on my face. "Hey."

I didn't know where her head was at, and I didn't want to rush anything either. "You got the text too?"

"Uhmm, yeah." Sommer rubbed the back of her neck nervously, looking around the garage in the process. "So, where we going?"

"Upstairs to see what's going on with my brother."

Reno charged into the parking garage, still on ten as he stormed across the pavement. "Matteo!"

My little brother just pushed my timeline back, but the point was we still had time. "Lil' bro, what's good?"

"Shit. Just had to chump ya mans off, but I'm good."

"What happened?" Sommer's voice behind me sent chills up my spine; no woman had that effect on me, EVER.

"Hey, sis. So I call this nigga up here because doc admitted Tamra for monitoring—"

"What! She not due yet!" Sommer rubbed our baby bump worriedly.

"Right. I said the same thing. We came up here 'cause she cramping, said something didn't feel right. They put him on the lil' machine, and *blam*! He got an arrythmia."

"Where did he get that from?" I stroked my beard, trying to focus on Reno but wanting to take Sommer in my arms so she knew I loved her and her only. Fuck Keedra.

"Nobody knows. You know doc say, 'oh, sometimes these things happen and correct themselves.'"

"Yeah, they gotta tell you that so they don't get sued." I spoke up.

"Not necessarily," Sommer interrupted. "Sometimes those things do happen with babies and correct themselves before the baby is out."

"Anyway, I text the nigga X, tell him to slide through so we can chat. Even if it wasn't about the baby being mine, I just wanted him to know where his girl at, right?"

"Right." Me and Sommer responded in unison.

"Soon as I text this clown, he walk in the room like he been there the whole time! I'm looking at him crazy, meanwhile, Tamra turned white as snow. So now I'm like, 'Ok, this nigga got her scared.' NOW I'M INTRIGUED. I start talking, nigga put his hand up and fucking shushes me like I'm some lil' ass kid!"

"Whaaaat!" I don't know who the fuck he thought we were, but Xander ain't bout to be shushing my little brother.

"RIGHT! THAT'S WHAT I SAID! I tell this nigga we need to talk, he turn to Tamra and say, 'I know you ain't been out here hoeing around with these Marino niggas.' You know it was up from there for me, nurse bust in the room and put both us out, tell us to get out the hospital before she have us arrested…yadda, yadda, yadda."

"What X doing while she talking?" I wanted to know.

"X staring at me like he wanna do something, so you know me, I'm like, 'what's good, my nigga?' Nurse tell us I can't beat the fuck outta him in the hospital since a baby's LIFE is at stake. You know I'm already on go mode; I'm 'bout to go back in the room, and this nigga X SWINGS ON ME!"

"He what?"

"YES MATTEO! YA BOY SWUNG ON ME! I duck, he end up putting his fist through the wall, and I pieced him up real quick before security escorted his dumb ass out the hospital."

"You good?"

"I'm good. Can't believe he said that to her though. I'm 'bout to go in here now and get some information from her. She gotta tell me something; X ain't the nigga she need to be scared of when she carrying my son."

"Facts. Where he at now?"

"I don't know," Reno kept looking around the garage for some odd reason, as if he had a specific purpose. "Tryna see if that raggedly ass Scat out here, cause I'm bout to put his big ass in the trunk, on foe 'nem!"

"I didn't see him, but give me a minute and we'll look for his ass together, aight?"

Reno looked back and forth between me and the second love of my life and nodded, walking back towards the elevator. "I'm starting from the top and working my way down, bro. Get at me when you can, aight?"

"I got'chu bro."

Sommer watched Reno until the elevator doors closed before she turned her attention back to me. "Is this a setup? Because if it is—"

Rubbing my hands together, I invaded her personal space and stood as close to her without us touching as I could. "You think I need to set you up, Dr. Park? We're in a hospital parking garage, give me some credit for coming up with something more original."

She dropped her head and chuckled sadly before taking a deep breath in and blowing it out hard, focusing on me a second time. "Matteo, what—"

Scrolling through my phone, I pulled up the Tidal app and found the perfect song that would fix us. Even if it didn't, she couldn't say I didn't try. The guitar rift from the opening instrumental played softly through the small speaker on my iPhone, her head lifted for a second as she watched me. *Gangsters don't do this shit.* Just as I was about to turn off the app, I saw the tears well up in her eyes. Could I live without this woman? Did I want to? The answer to those questions gave me the incentive I needed drop down on one knee and took her hand in mine:

Talk…let's have conversations in the dark

World is sleeping, I'm awake with you, with you

Watch movies that we've both already seen

I ain't even looking at the screen
It's true, I got my eyes on you
And you say that you're not worthy
You get hung up on your flaws
Well, in my eyes, you are as perfect as you are

Staring in her eyes, nothing else mattered to me other than her as I sang John Legend's 'Conversations In The Dark' to the woman who still wore both my rings, even though she wasn't speaking to me. The only woman in the world who mattered to me more than my mother. The only woman I almost threw it all away over someone who meant nothing to me, even before the day I tossed her out my house. I was too blind to see how much I loved her and she loved me until I experienced a moment when I almost lost her. I reached up and wiped her tears while I continued to serenade my one true love:

I won't ever try to change you, change you

I will always want the same you, same you

> *Swear on everything I pray to*
> *That I won't break your heart...*

Sommer crouched down beside me and wrapped her arms around my neck, showering my face with kisses before she gave me those lips back. "I love you, Matteo Marino. I love you so much," she blubbered between kisses.

"I love you too, Dr. Sommer Park. I love you and I'm sorry. Keedra don't mean nothing—"

"After today, we won't ever mention her name again, Matteo. She doesn't exist in the space we created, you and me."

"Long as I got you by my side, nothing else matters. Besides my brother and my nephew, that is," I kissed her tears away as I spoke.

"Oh my God, your nephew and your brother!" she expressed happily. "That's our whole reason for being here!"

"Let me see where he at." I grabbed my phone and hit talk on his number, hoping he was on his way back to the second floor where we were.

Sommer shook her head laughing, no doubt at Reno's story from earlier about him and X. "Be good, Matteo."

"Baby, I'm always good, whatchu' talking about?"

"I'm not playing with you, Matteo. Be good."

"I will." I leaned over and pecked her on the cheek before sliding between them full lips a second time. "Why you taste like pineapples?"

"Because I got a husband," she smiled back. "Wives supposed to taste tropical."

"I'll keep that in mind next time I—"

"Bye, Matteo." She mushed my head and walked towards the garage steps.

"Where you going, pretty girl?"

"Matteo, I did my residency here. ProHealth is like home for me, I can't tell you how many times I've ran up and down these steps tryna wake up. Sometimes old habits die hard," she shot me that smile I still see in my sleep.

"Aight Dr. Park. Gon' inside and I'll be up as soon as me and Reno take care of this business with X."

"Ok."

Sommer

Staring at Matteo's gorgeous lips, I got that familiar tingle between my thighs as he expressed his love for me through John Legend's words. He knew I loved that song, and it was fitting for what we were currently going through. Laying in my bed when the text from Reno came through, I got up and didn't give it a second thought as I pulled on pants and a shirt, heading to the first hospital I worked at out of grad school.

When I stepped out of my car in that garage and saw his face, memories of me and him together came full force and inundated my mental. The things Matteo did to my body was bananas, I couldn't get enough of him and vice versa. As the awkward pause settle between us, I visually raped him, remembering a trip we took to Green Bay a few weeks prior:

"I grew up in Wisconsin and never been to Green Bay." Me and Matteo went to the city because I said I was bored, three hours later we were in the midst of chasing each other on Segways downtown when we were supposed to be doing a scavenger hunt.

"Never?"

"Never. As a matter of fact, what do you know about the city? I thought you and your brothers were from Milwaukee."

"We used to fuck with this one nigga—"

"Matteo!"

"What?"

"Language? Not all black men are niggas."

"Baby, you know that's just how I talk. I ain't mean no harm."

"I'm saying, you should—"

"Aht-aht. I don't walk in the clinic telling you how to treat your patients, do I?"

"No, but—"

"This who I was when you met me. It's a problem now?"

I sighed because he was right. I might not have liked the word, but I fell in love with Matteo for who he was, language and all. Last thing I wanted to do was change him. "Continue."

"Like I was saying, we used to fuck with this one promoter up here named Quentin who used to cop dope from us on the side. Once he got that bag up, he got out the game and bought a club. He good people though."

I munched on the pineapples he grabbed from Whole Foods when I told him I needed a healthy snack to tide me over until dinner. "Are we seeing him while we're here?"

"Nah. I'm seeing you while we here," Matteo replied as he held the door to our room at the Hampton Inn open for me. I crossed the threshold and he grabbed a *handful of my ass in the process. "You think I fed you all those pineapples because I thought you was hungry?"*

"To be honest, yea. Why else would you stuff me full of tropical fruit?" I replied playfully, cheesing while allowing the strap from my dress to fall off my shoulder.

He grabbed my waist and pulled me closer to where he stood in the middle of the room. "Let me show you." Locking his lips around mine, Matteo allowed his right hand to explore my curves and linger at the hem of my dress. I'd gained a few extra pounds thanks to the baby and even though I was a doctor, sometimes felt ashamed because of it. On those days my man reassured me that he loved every curve, every dimple, every cushion on every inch of my body. "Wit'cho thick ass. You so fuckin' beautiful, Sommer."

Cupping my face, we continued our kiss as his hand travelled up my dress and gripped my upper thighs. Without warning, he dropped to his knees and dove underneath the thin material, snatching my panties to indulge in my pussy lips. I grabbed the back of his head as he raised my leg and draped it around his neck.
"Matteo—"

"You like that, baby?" he mumbled, humming on my pearl.

"Mmhmm," I nodded as he inserted two fingers inside my pussy. The explosion he loved to chase began to tickle my spine, my eyes closed once my leg started wobbling.

"Gimme that sweetness baby. Cum for Daddy," he breathed into my sex, rubbing his goatee against my inner thighs and I released all over his face. Matteo lapped every drop, his tongue felt so good I became lightheaded. He caught me before I fainted

and carried me over to the small couch in the corner. "Is my baby ok?"

"I'm fine. But I can think of one thing that would be better though," I smiled, reaching for his belt buckle.

"Nah, you good. I keep forgetting you still not used to my tongue game, even after all this time. You carrying my baby though, so I got the rest of our lives to train you on it."

I moved to unfasten his pants, the perverted part of me loved his pretty dick that curved slightly to the left like a hook. My second best friend popped out the minute his zipper came down and I squeezed the base while looking in my lover's eyes.

"Boy, bye." I turned my lips, lying through my teeth. Matteo's mouth game could put me to sleep faster than the D.

"You say that, but you can't take it when I do something freaky to your ass though.

Act like you don't like when I spread them legs and have that pussy cumming like a waterfall before I give you the dick. Watch what happen." Matteo mumbled huskily in my ear while stroking my kitty, he already had me cumming instantly at the thought. "Told you," he uttered softly, sliding his pants off before he gave me all his love for the rest of the night.

I was so focused on my trip down memory lane that I didn't see the red Buick speeding toward me as I crossed the street until it was too late…

Keedra

When Matteo called and said we needed to talk, I was positive he was gonna ask me to move back in. With everything going wrong in my life, knowing he was still thinking about me let me know I had his heart. He was only with Sommer out of guilt for being the reason I killed her twin. If he really was upset, I would be in jail or worse.

My mother was serious this time when she told me to get out. I came back to my clothes thrown across her front yard ripped into shreds. I called the police on her, enough was enough. I didn't have the money to buy all new things; if anything now I had to put a roof over my head. The police escorted me inside the house where I found out she stole the money I put up for me to move. All $7,000 of my money was gone. Then this bitch had the nerve to tell the police I was lying and I ain't have no money because I didn't have a job. Since I couldn't prove it, I had to take the L.

I'd been going back and forth staying in shelters, but lately each one I went to claimed they didn't have room. I'd been sleeping in the back seat of my car for about a week now, and with this baby growing bigger by the day I needed room to move around. I needed some help, and not from either off my parents. Off the top of my head, the only other person I could think of besides Jerry that would cash me out was Ronnie. I hadn't seen him in a while, and I knew his mother would be too happy seeing my baby bump. I called him up and he answered on the second ring:

"Hey babe!" Silence. "Ronnie?"

"Mmm… ssss… right there, baby," a woman's voice cooed in the background. "She can't do this, can she?"

"Oh—ooohhh, naw. She don't do that," Ronnie's voice replied. "I told you we ain't engaged for real, that shit was for my mama."

"Well, now that yo' mama know you like dick, SHE CAN GO NOW!" The voice's cadence changed from a high alto to a deep bass. "Yeah, that's right, bitch! I know you on the phone and you blocked now! BLING! BOOM! BUH-BYE BITCH!"

Tears welled up in my eyes as the phone slid to the floor with a dull thump. First Matteo, then my own mother, my father basically told me he wanted to keep fucking me knowing I was his daughter, and now trade had his bitch dump me over the phone. We not gonna even mention the fact Luca stopped answering his phone for me, at the very least I thought we were friends. These past few weeks had been rough; even as an only child I'd never felt so alone in my life.

"Wait… David! I wonder if he's still in the States," I mumbled, fumbling for my phone. Finding his number I hit talk, praying he was here and in a good mood. I sent up a small prayer to whoever listened when he answered.

"Hey… Keedra?"

"Hi, David. How are you?"

"Uhmm… a little shocked right now, but that's neither here nor there."

"Shocked? What happened?'

"Just found out I have a son."

I rubbed my baby bump worriedly; David was also a potential father for this child. As much as I hoped it was Matteo's, I ultimately had to face the reality of my situation. "Oh, wow! How is the mother doing?"

"She died twenty-two years ago." David's voice sounded far away, further than our little corner of Wisconsin.

"How is that possible?"

David seemed to snap out of his daze; I wondered what that was all about. "Never mind. So what's going on with you?"

"Funny you mention you have a son," I continued to drag my hand in semicircles around my belly. "We really need to talk."

"Sure. When would you like to chat?"

"Tonight?" If I could get some money out of him today, I wouldn't have to sleep in my car again tonight.

"Ehhh… tonight might not be a good idea."

"Oh, are you out of the country?"

"No, no, I'm in Wisconsin. I'm gonna try and get in contact with my son while I'm here. Maybe we'll go out for dinner or something, I don't know."

"Want me to come too? I can be your moral support, just in case. Plus I'd love to meet your son."

"Oh, no, that won't be necessary. I don't want Sommer to be uncomfortable; I never implied I was in a relationship with anyone when we met."

"Sommer?"

"Yes, Sommer. My son's wife."

"Your—your son wouldn't be Matteo Marino, is he?"

"Yes, you know him?"

Oh my God... not again... "David, I gotta let you go. Give me a call later, ok?"

"Take care, Keedra." He hurried off the phone, not even acknowledging my request.

I slammed my phone against the passenger side door and screamed until my throat was sore. Wetness spilled freely from my orbs and flooded down my cheeks in rapid succession. What had I done in a former life that would make God treat me like this? All the men in this damn city... what were the odds I'd have sex not just with my own brother, but my father, my boyfriend, his brothers, *and* his father too? And if that wasn't bad enough, I was pregnant with no idea of who this child's father was. True enough this baby wasn't Duffy's, but for what it was worth I would've been better off if he was in the running too. At least he would've made sure I was good, unlike the rest of these selfish bastards.

With my current situation being what it was, I almost called my mother back and apologized, but in hindsight, I wouldn't give that bitch the satisfaction. She thought she broke me, but this time I wasn't running back home to hide under her titty. *Oh, you hate me, huh? Bet I have the last laugh this time, you toxic bitch.*

Out of nowhere, a sharp pain shot through my side, doubling me over in agony. I reached out to turn the key in the ignition, but a second throbbing wave crippled my body from the waist down. Frantically, I looked around for my phone to call for help, but noticed it fell between the seat. The pain subsided enough for my fingertips to caress the smooth screen before antagonizing me a third time. I rolled my window down to scream for help when I felt a wet stickiness between my thighs. "Help me…" my raggedy whisper expressed to the universe before my lower body went into spasms again. I closed my eyes and wept as time stood still; for reasons that would forever be unknown to me, my body was beginning to reject the life growing inside me.

The street I was parked on was quiet… too quiet. Quiet enough for no one to hear my pleas for assistance, quiet enough for my baby to begin his premature escape from my womb, quiet enough for me to realize my child was slipping away and there was nothing I could do to stop it. Never would I hear his or her little cries. Never would I hold him or her in my arms. Never would I have someone who loved me unconditionally for being me. Never would I know the feeling of pure love, *real* love from a small human who looked at me with nothing but true love, not the superficial love I knew all too well. *Oh God, please… please send someone to help me…*

When I opened my eyes, the cramping had subsided, but there was still a small puddle between my legs. Instinctively, I knew I had to go to the hospital. With no prenatal care…plus knowing I was still drinking in the clubs every night, I knew there was nothing that could be done to save the baby at this point. I'd had a D&C done before when I had some abnormal bleeding, but this time the surgical procedure would be to remove the remnants of my child. That's all my baby was reduced to at this point—remnants. Remnants of what might have been. Remnants of a life lost. Remnants of a future that now would never be. Remnants…

The sun was setting by the time I pulled up to ProHealth Memorial in Waukesha and I was tired, both physically and mentally. With everything that transpired in the past couple of hours, I still had to get out of the car and make my way to the emergency room alone. As I drove towards the circular driveway to park hopefully a little closer, I thought my eyes were deceiving me when I saw… *her*.

Sommer.

The bitch who stole my man and my life.

Oh she's happy, huh?

She's *happy*.

Everything became a blur as I focused in on her round baby bump that she had the nerve to reach out and rub as she took her time crossing the street. She knew I was coming to this hospital. She knew what she was doing.

Taunting me.

Mocking me.

Why else would she be here?

What about me, bitch! What about my baby!

Her body hit the front of my car first, flipping across the hood and landing on my windshield as her surprised glare haunted me through the glass. Blood covered her face, her eyes agape and focused on nothing for a second longer before slowly closing shut. She didn't even see me coming.

Bitches bleed just like us, Sommer. I'll kill a pregnant hoe too.

Notice I didn't type 'The End' or 'To Be Continued'. This story was supposed to end with two books, but sometimes these characters take on a mind of their own. I've seen the posts where readers say the story could've ended after part 2. Is there a part 3? Come on now, y'all know me better than that. I'll let y'all determine whether I drop it or not. Drop the review on Amazon and let me know.

Part 1: https://amzn.to/3xRsF1b

Do you have IG? Follow me:

http://instagram.com/fatima_munroe

Got Twitter? Me too:

http://twitter.com/fatima_munroe

What else am I working on? Funny you should ask…keep scrolling!

Kissed: Purpose and Nadir's Story

"Hello?" I didn't bother looking at the screen, if someone was calling me at two o'clock in the morning it must've been important.

"Hey, uhm Nadir?"

"This is Nadir."

"Hey Nadir, this is Purpose."

I paused for a second, not knowing what to say. "Uhm, hey Purpose. Is everything ok?"

"Yea, yea, everything's fine. I was just calling because—," she held the phone for a few seconds, "because I didn't get my schedule before I left work. Can you tell me if I work tomorrow or not?"

"Uhh, I don't have the schedule right in front of me, but I think you're off."

"Ok, thanks," she didn't hang up right away.

"Purpose?"

"Yea?"

"I know this might be a little forward of me, but are you busy tomorrow?"

"No, why?"

"I just wanted to know if—,"

"You need me to pick up a shift?" she questioned hopefully.

"No, not that. You know what Purpose? I'm gonna stop beating around the bush with you. I'm attracted to you like a muthafucka, you sexy as fuck to me."

"Nadir, I can't believe you just said that to me!" she feigned shock

"Well, I know you didn't call me at two o'clock in the morning to ask me about your shift when you could've just called the job in the morning. Tell me you not attracted to me too."

"I'm—I'm not," she whispered in my ear.

"Tell you what then. I'm about to text you my address. If you wanna stop lying to yourself, I'll see you when you get here. If you wanna keep lying to yourself, then I'll see you at work, and this never happened."

"Nadir I got—," I heard her voice before I hung up. I wasn't gonna play these grade school, 'do-you-like-me-circle-yes-or-no' games with her. Texting the addy, I went and hopped in the shower; I had to make sure I smelled good before she got here.

Once I stepped out of the shower, I straightened up a bit; my house wasn't dirty, but I needed to load the dishwasher and turn it on. Lighting some incense in the kitchen and a vanilla scented candle downstairs, I checked my iPhone to see if she read my message. She had.

The ringing of the doorbell made me smile, nobody 'just stopped by' my home at

2:45 in the morning unless they were invited. I opened the door to see Purpose standing there in a white silk robe and ballerina shoes with slippers in her hand.

"Thought you weren't attracted to me," I smirked as she switched her round ass across the threshold.

"I'm not," she chuckled, kicking off her shoes and sliding into her slippers. "I wasn't doing nothing else though, so I figured why not?"

"That's what you figured, huh," I closed the door behind her and walked to where she sat on the couch with her robe slightly opened. "Let me see what you got under that robe, since you figurin'."

"Oh, you mean this old thing?" she smiled as she shimmied her left shoulder from underneath the sheath. Her BARE left shoulder, might I add. "You know how the old saying goes: ain't nothing open at 3 a.m.

but legs." Checking her Apple Watch, she looked back at me with a sly smirk. "Know what time it is, Nadir?"

I guess that's enough for now. Wait…you said a sneak peek of Part 3? Y'all know what to do…

Weak For A Coldhearted Goon 3

unedited

Matteo

I hated hospitals. Sommer watched as her
sister slipped away right in front of her eyes;
I'll never forget the hurt and pain she went
through from that. Before she got there that
day, the doctor said Shannie's chances of
survival were bleak, yet there was still a
possibility she could recover. When her
body went into convulsions in front of her
sister, I knew he was lying.

The ear-splitting whine of the ambulance
sounded as if it was sitting on the street. I
was facing the opposite direction; I didn't
want to see any more sick people than I

needed to. Granted, I would be there when lil' bro had his first, but until then…no thanks.

Where this nigga at? I hit talk on his information once it popped up on the Bluetooth. It didn't take that long to find a big nigga like X. "Reno—"

"Matteo—man…" Reno's voice never sounded like he was right now. I take that back, anytime someone mentioned Pop…

"What happened to your lil' man, bro?" I walked through the garage with my head down once I heard his voice. With Luca gone, it was a blessing knowing we'd have another Marino man in the family, now…

"It…it ain't him, man."

"What's wrong with ya' voice then, bro? You sound fucked up." I walked across the street, shaking my head at the police cars and detectives blocking the entire block from corner to corner. *What happened out here?* "Where's Sommer?"

"That's what I was calling you about, bro. Sommer…"

"Sommer what?" I moved quickly to the hospital's sliding doors; I needed to get to her. "Where is she?"

"Bro, that's what I'm trying to tell you. She got hit by a car while she was walking—"

"She got—" I stopped, because I felt the rage inside moving rapidly to the surface. I had to get the information from my brother before I went on a killing spree. "Where you at, Reno?"

"In the trauma center waiting room. Doc said they need her next of kin to sign off on some paperwork. I was just about to call you."

I put him on hold as I stormed to the receptionist's desk. "Where the fuck—" I stopped, seeing the scared look on her face. Dropping my head for a second, I closed my eyes and took two deep breaths like Sommer made me do whenever I got upset. It wasn't the receptionist fault some asshole had a death wish; this woman was just doing her job. "Can you tell me where the trauma center waiting room is, please?" I asked as steadily as I could considering the circumstances.

"Yes. Take this hallway all the way down and buzz the door marked Authorized Staff Only Allowed Beyond This Point. I'll call ahead and let them know you're on your way, Mr.—"

"Marino. Matteo Marino. My wife Sommer was hit by a car and—"

"Oh, the lady that got hit right out here about twenty minutes ago? My thoughts and prayers are with you, Mr. Marino. I saw the whole thing and—"

"You saw the whole thing?" My interest was piqued at this point, I had a witness. "Have they talked to you yet?" I questioned with a raised eyebrow, sliding my eyes to the door and back.

"Uhmm...not yet."

"Just tell me what the car looked like, that's all."

"Late model Buick. Red, looked like four doors..."

I know this bitch didn't... "With a rust spot on the passenger side door?"

"Yes. I think it was a woman behind the wheel. I called the emergency room as soon as I saw the impact."

"Thank you. When they ask, tell them you came out the bathroom and saw her on the ground, that's when you made the call." I peeled off a few hundreds and passed them to her. "Are there cameras monitoring the outside?"

"Yea, but security is gone for the day," she lowered her voice, leaning in my direction. "I know somebody that can probably get you that video and pretend like the system was broke when they ask."

"If you can, it's a thousand dollars in it for you too," I mumbled lowly while looking around for anyone who might be listening in on our conversation. "Have them come get me when you got something, aight?"

"Ok."

"Good look." I tapped the desk twice and walked towards the trauma center. Each step I took became heavier as my heart dropped to my feet. This bitch Keedra didn't know when to quit, obviously. With Reno up here and X chilling in the trunk of his own car in the parking garage, this was something I had to go get my hands dirty for. I was gonna see what the doctors was talking about first, then after that...

By the time I got to the door the receptionist was talking about, it was already buzzing for me to enter. I spotted my brother talking to the doctor with his phone in hand and remembered I forgot to hang up with him. He noticed me and they both headed over in my direction. "Doc, this is Matteo, my brother."

"Nice to meet you, Mr. Marino." The older African-American man shook my hand with a grave look in his eyes. "Such a shame it had to be under these circumstances."

"I agree. Can you give me an update on my wife's condition? My brother was saying you needed some paperwork signed?"

"Ahem...yes." Doc cleared his throat a few times before he spoke. "These cases are always very difficult for the family, but we also have to follow the proper protocol.

Your wife has a broken wrist, three cracked ribs, and a contusion on her skull. Because she suffered a head injury, we've placed her into a medically induced coma so her body can heal itself. As far as we can tell, the baby survived the impact. Your wife's motherly instinct kicked in at some point; she was found with her arms around her pelvis, therefore lessening the impact on the fetus. However, that type of trauma caused Mrs. Marino to experience pre-term labor, right now she's about five centimeters dilated. We need your permission to extract the baby from her womb, or we can try to stop the labor, which I wouldn't advise at this stage."

"Do whatever you need to do to save my son, doc," I responded, staring blankly in the distance.

"Your daughter, you mean?"

"Daughter?" *I could very easily be carrying Shannie Celeste Marino too. I put in some work myself that night...* Sommer's words ran through my head as I rubbed my hands across my waves. "Can I see my wife?"

"Normally we wouldn't allow it, but just for a few minutes," the doctor nodded his approval, leading me to where my wife laid covered in bandages. "Talk to her, man. She can hear you, talk to your woman. I'll have that paperwork ready when you come out, aight?" Doc patted my shoulder before closing the door behind him.

I was at a total loss for words. She looked so innocent, so delicate. My eyes wandered over the small figure lying peacefully on the bed asleep and covered completely from her chin downward. "Sommer..." my voice wavered for a second as my mind flooded with memories of our good times.

"I know who did this to you. I'm going to take care of that, trust me, baby. She not gonna get away with this. And the baby…you was right. It's a girl. A girl who needs her mama. We both need you, Sommer…"

"Hey, baby daddy. You ready?"

"Baby daddy, huh?" I leaned in and kissed her neck, checking out the outfit she had on. Sommer looked sexy as hell as always, dressed in an all-white, form-fitting dress that hugged her like a glove, showing off our baby bump. I'd just bought the gray Dolce and Gabbana leather biker jacket hanging around her shoulders while we were on our way back from Atlanta, only because she convinced me it matched her gray stilettos perfectly. Sommer knew I loved her hair straight down her back, and I promptly ran my fingers through her strands.

"I don't recall saying 'I do', so that makes you my baby daddy." She kissed my lips before heading for the truck. I ran ahead of her and grabbed her door, making sure she was comfortable.

"So I get yo' lil' dusty ass seven carats, and that don't mean shit, huh?" I hit the push button start and pulled out the driveway.

"Seven carats? This a cubic zirconia, boy what'chu talking about?" She raised her hand and wiggled her fingers while disconnecting my phone from the Bluetooth.

"This ain't." I reached in my pocket and passed her a ring box. Pulling over on the side of the road, I leaned over and wiped the tears streaming down her face. "Oh, now we quiet, huh?" I grinned, watching as her hand shook slightly.

"Matteo... you make me so sick." She opened the box slowly and got the shock of *her life when she saw the new ring I got for her. "This is so beautiful, baby."*

"Am I baby daddy, or am I baby? I'm confused, big mama." I took the box from her and took the ring out, sliding the deep blue sapphire set in a platinum band on top of the two carat white pear diamond I originally gave her when I proposed. My jeweler was out of town, and that was all I had access to at the moment.

"You baby. You my baby, Matteo," Sommer showered me with kisses before she tried to climb over the armrest, but Junior stopped all that. "I'll thank you when we get to the house..."

"Sommer, listen to me. The doctor said they gotta take the baby..." A still tear sat quietly in the crevice of her eye before breaking free to roll undisturbed down her cheek. With the crook of my finger, I reached out and gently wiped it away. "I'm gonna be here until they give me an update on you and my princess, then I'll be back, ok? I promise I'll be back, Sommer." I kissed her forehead as a soft tap on the door interrupted our moment. Normally I'd tell whoever was disturbing me to get out, but these people were here to take care of the two most important women to me. "Here I come."

The door cracked open slightly before the nurse peeked her head in. "Mr. Marino, it's time."

"Aight." I closed my eyes and focused on peace and clarity. Sommer told me that's what helped her cope with her sister's passing. I knew that wasn't her fate; if it was, I'd know. "Love you." I kissed her head again before walking out of her room and heading to the waiting room to…wait.

*Thanks for rocking with me, I
appreciate you!*

Fatima M.

Made in the USA
Columbia, SC
24 April 2023